**MEN** *in* **UNIFORM**

**Courteous, courageous and commanding—**
these heroes lay it all on the line for the
people they love in more than fifty stories about
loyalty, bravery and romance.
**Don't miss a single one!**

### AVAILABLE FEBRUARY 2010
*A Vow to Love* by Sherryl Woods
*Serious Risks* by Rachel Lee
*Who Do You Love?* by Maggie Shayne and Marilyn Pappano
*Dear Maggie* by Brenda Novak
*A Randall Returns* by Judy Christenberry
*Informed Risk* by Robyn Carr
*Five-Alarm Affair* by Marie Ferrarella

### AVAILABLE MARCH 2010
*The Man from Texas* by Rebecca York
*Mistaken Identity* by Merline Lovelace
*Bad Moon Rising* by Kathleen Eagle
*Moriah's Mutiny* by Elizabeth Bevarly
*Have Gown, Need Groom* by Rita Herron
*Heart of the Tiger* by Lindsay McKenna

### AVAILABLE APRIL 2010
*Landry's Law* by Kelsey Roberts
*Love at First Sight* by B.J. Daniels
*The Sheriff of Shelter Valley* by Tara Taylor Quinn
*A Match for Celia* by Gina Wilkins
*That's Our Baby!* by Pamela Browning
*Baby, Our Baby!* by Patricia Thayer

**AVAILABLE MAY 2010**

*Special Assignment: Baby* by Debra Webb
*My Baby, My Love* by Dani Sinclair
*The Sheriff's Proposal* by Karen Rose Smith
*The Marriage Conspiracy* by Christine Rimmer
*The Woman for Dusty Conrad* by Tori Carrington
*The White Night* by Stella Bagwell
*Code Name: Prince* by Valerie Parv

**AVAILABLE JUNE 2010**

*Same Place, Same Time* by C.J. Carmichael
*One Last Chance* by Justine Davis
*By Leaps and Bounds* by Jacqueline Diamond
*Too Many Brothers* by Roz Denny Fox
*Secretly Married* by Allison Leigh
*Strangers When We Meet* by Rebecca Winters

**AVAILABLE JULY 2010**

*Babe in the Woods* by Caroline Burnes
*Serving Up Trouble* by Jill Shalvis
*Deputy Daddy* by Carla Cassidy
*The Major and the Librarian* by Nikki Benjamin
*A Family Man* by Mindy Neff
*The President's Daughter* by Annette Broadrick
*Return to Tomorrow* by Marisa Carroll

**AVAILABLE AUGUST 2010**

*Remember My Touch* by Gayle Wilson
*Return of the Lawman* by Lisa Childs
*If You Don't Know by Now* by Teresa Southwick
*Surprise Inheritance* by Charlotte Douglas
*Snowbound Bride* by Cathy Gillen Thacker
*The Good Daughter* by Jean Brashear

**AVAILABLE SEPTEMBER 2010**

*The Hero's Son* by Amanda Stevens
*Secret Witness* by Jessica Andersen
*On Pins and Needles* by Victoria Pade
*Daddy in Dress Blues* by Cathie Linz
*AKA: Marriage* by Jule McBride
*Pregnant and Protected* by Lilian Darcy

MEN
*in*
UNIFORM

*USA TODAY* Bestselling Author

# KELSEY ROBERTS

## LANDRY'S LAW

# HARLEQUIN®

TORONTO • NEW YORK • LONDON
AMSTERDAM • PARIS • SYDNEY • HAMBURG
STOCKHOLM • ATHENS • TOKYO • MILAN • MADRID
PRAGUE • WARSAW • BUDAPEST • AUCKLAND

Recycling programs
for this product may
not exist in your area.

ISBN-13: 978-0-373-36260-8

LANDRY'S LAW

Copyright © 2000 by Rhonda Harding Pollero

Many thanks to Dr. Harry Sernaker,
Dr. Christopher Galuardi, Dr. Lew Schon and
Dr. Wendy Spencer. Because of these talented
professionals, I can walk. Thanks also to my dear
husband, Bob, who has been there for me all
during this ordeal. Much love and thanks to all!

# *Prologue*

Snow crunched beneath his boots as Sheriff Seth Landry cautiously made his way down the steep bank to the crime scene. Flurries still swirled in the air as he greeted his deputy, J. D. Lindsey.

"Has the coroner been called?"

J.D. nodded, then blew warm breath into his cupped hands. "As far as I know, no one has touched a thing."

"Who called it in?" Seth asked.

J.D. pointed toward the Mountainview Inn behind them. "One of the guests. Ken Updyke. He's passing through on his way to Seattle. He was out jogging and came up on this."

Seth regarded the scene. The snowstorm had

pretty much obliterated the area around the body. He stepped forward and knelt to get a better look at the victim. Judging from the small entrance wound at the back of the guy's head, Seth figured the weapon was a .22.

He also noted that the man's clothing wasn't right. He was wearing a suit beneath a camouflage down jacket but didn't have any gloves on. He made a mental note of that inconsistency.

"Looks just like the last one," J.D. remarked.

Seth's gut knotted at the mere suggestion. Jasper, Montana was a small, out-of-the-way town where everyone knew everyone else. Tourists passed through to visit some of the quaint shops and historic markers in the area. To date, none of them had turned out to be serial killers. *If* he actually had a serial killer on his hands.

"Anyone know who he is?" Seth asked the half-dozen or so onlookers who had gathered. The victim was on his stomach, but his face was turned to one side.

"Isn't that Harvey Whitlock?" one of them asked.

Seth adjusted his position and tilted his head to get a better look. "It appears so."

"He's only lived here a couple of months," J.D. said. "I guess that's long enough to make an enemy."

Seth stood as the coroner arrived. He shook hands with Dr. Hall. "Sorry to get you out so early," Seth offered as he watched the doctor shifting from one foot to the other in an apparent attempt to ward off the cold.

"I'm getting too old for this," Hall grumbled. "Isn't that Harvey Whitlock?"

Seth nodded. Dr. Hall handed J.D. a camera and instructed him on where and when to take photographs of the victim and the scene.

The idea that there might me some deranged killer running loose in his town still distracted Seth. He pulled out his notepad and started making some observations and listing possibilities.

By the time Dr. Hall was ready to have the officers turn the body over, the ambulance crew and at least a dozen more gawkers had arrived. Seth silently hoped his death would be more private. Not some public spectacle like poor Harvey's.

J.D. took the feet, the ambulance guys the mid-section, and Seth took the head. With practiced precision, they turned Harvey over so that he could be placed on a stretcher, then whisked away from the prying, curious eyes of the crowd.

"What's that?" Seth asked, pointing to Harvey's left palm.

They all moved in for a closer look. The frigid water from the creek had washed away the writing until it was very faint.

"Savannah, 9-1-2," Seth read aloud.

"Looks like part of a phone number. Maybe an area code?" J.D. theorized, excitedly.

Seth was puzzled. If he recalled correctly, Harvey was from someplace in the east, which had 200, 300 and 400 area codes. He breathed a little easier. There had been no writing on the hand of the first victim. Maybe the two cases weren't related.

"I don't think that's a phone number," came a voice from the crowd.

Seth turned and looked in the direction of the voice. It was a man in his early thirties. He had the dress and manner of a yuppie tourist. Seth went over to the man.

"Why not?"

The yuppie shrugged. "I saw him last night in the bar."

"And?" Seth prompted.

"He was staring at the clock."

"When was this?" Seth asked.

"Maybe ten after nine or so."

"And you're sure it was him?"

The yuppie insisted that he was.

"How can you be so sure? You aren't a local."

"I remember him because of the *babe* who showed up to meet him. I mean, no offense to the dead or anything, but that guy isn't exactly *GQ* material, and he managed to snag the prettiest woman in the place."

"What did she look like?"

"Pretty brown hair, incredible green eyes, a body to die for—sorry, poor choice of words—I mean—"

"Did you happen to hear him call her by name?"

The yuppie nodded with enthusiasm. "That's why

I don't think that writing on his hand is a phone number."

"Because?" Seth prodded.

"Because he called the woman Savannah."

Seth swallowed, hard. *Savannah Wyatt.*

# Chapter One

Savannah Wyatt was armed for a sneak attack. Slowly, cautiously, she tiptoed across the cool wood floor, moving ever closer to her prey. Her victim didn't flinch. Didn't turn around in time to see her coming.

"Gotcha!" she exclaimed as she captured the field mouse between the floor and the box. Its days of stalking her dried goods for the better part of a week were history!

She could hear the little thing scurrying around under the box, clearly frightened and disoriented. She muttered a guilty curse and blew out a breath. The kitchen, where she had trapped the varmint, was a good twenty feet from the front door. She was less than three feet from the kitchen door, but a five-foot snowdrift blocked it. Silently, she said a few choice words about Montana in the grips of winter, none of them flattering.

Considering her options, Savannah tried to think of a way to grant the mouse freedom without actually touching it. One of the solutions she considered was barbecue tongs, but that would mean lifting the shoe box edge high enough for the furry little monster to make an escape, so that was abandoned.

Lifting her foot, she applied pressure, thus leaving her hands free to search for a way out of this mess.

Catching sight of herself in the stainless steel refrigerator, she decided she looked a tad like a brunette version of the painting of George Washington crossing the Delaware River by Larry Rivers. Shaking her head, Savannah reminded herself that art and fashion were her past. Her present was the very unglamorous job of liberating Mighty Mouse.

A knock reverberated through the two-room cabin.

"Enter at your own risk," Savannah called. She had stopped locking the door of the secluded cabin during the day after her first few desolate weeks in Jasper. Besides, it wasn't as if she had lots of strangers dropping in.

She smelled his inexpensive cologne a flash before she turned and saw Junior Baumgartner standing in the foyer, stomping snow from his boots

on a rag rug designed to save the finish on the wide
pine flooring from potential water damage. His
balding head was covered by a navy watch cap,
which was the same shade as his down parka. She
smiled at him. Frederick—known only as Junior
around Jasper—was a kind of friend. She worked
part-time for his mother and the two of them sort of
came as a package deal, in spite of the fact that
Junior had to be pushing forty.

As was his habit, he kept his eyes downcast when
he spoke. "What are you doing?"

"I was smart enough to trap a mouse but not smart
enough to know how to get rid of it once I did," she
replied in a rather self-deprecating tone.

"Want me to kill it?" Junior offered.

"Lord, no!" she fairly shouted. "I just want to put
him outside to fend for himself. Mice can live
outside in this kind of weather, right?"

Junior was about to respond when another knock
sounded at the door. The sound made Junior jump
nervously. Not for the first time, Savannah felt pangs
of compassion for the man. Though he was a
lifelong resident of the tight-knit ranching community, she seemed to be his only friend—unless you
counted his sweet but overbearing parent as a friend.
Savannah had learned her first day on the job that
Olive was Junior's friend, mentor, and fiercest pro-
tector. He spoke with a slight lisp and seemed incapable of making eye contact with anyone. Poor man.

She wondered what made him so shy, jumpy and awkward. Possibly his mother—it seemed as if the widowed Olive still hadn't cut the umbilical cord to her only child.

"Hey, Junior," came a friendly greeting that immediately set Savannah's teeth on edge.

Sheriff Seth Landry didn't take the time to shake the snow from his boots. He entered her small home, removing his hat as he came closer. *Too close,* her little voice screamed.

"Some new form of intense yoga, Miss Wyatt?" he asked with enough charm to melt her bones.

Which was exactly what she didn't like about this man. Two weeks earlier he'd all but accused her of murdering Richard Fowler. Now he was sauntering in as if he'd been invited for afternoon tea.

"Sheriff," she acknowledged evenly.

"Junior?" Seth said as he opened the buttons on his leather uniform jacket. "I need some time alone with Miss Wyatt."

"But I have to help her with the mouse," Junior protested almost forcefully. "Besides, she didn't kill that Fowler man and you should leave her alone."

She was surprised to hear Junior so adamant, but then again, she knew he liked her and was probably just being chivalrous. The sheriff didn't seem to notice or care that he had upset Junior.

She watched Seth's inky-black eyes go from Junior's up-turned red face to the box she was guarding with the weight of her foot. "I'll take care of the mouse," Seth assured Junior. "You go on home now, but be careful out on the highway. Those roads are mighty slick."

"Yes, sir," Junior said, deflated, then in a brighter tone he added, "Bye, Savannah."

"Bye, Junior," she called over her shoulder. To Seth, she said, "Do your civic duty. Please."

"Where's the top of the box?" Seth asked, shrugging out of his jacket.

Savannah's mind threatened to go blank as she took in his broad shoulders, trim waist and uniform. She never would have pegged herself as a sucker for a man in uniform, but she was wrong. Seth Landry was an incredible blend of dark, dangerous and delightful. Too bad her life in Jasper was temporary.

*Too bad he hasn't technically cleared me as a suspect in Richard Fowler's murder.*

"The top?" Seth prompted.

"On—on the bed," she stammered.

Being in Savannah's bedroom made Seth a little uncomfortable. What should have been an investigation was quickly turning into an inventory. The room was neat as a pin and incredibly feminine. The subtle scent of flowers hung in the air. Candles adorned nearly every inch of the bedroom and what he could see of the open bathroom. Even though he knew better, he could just imagine the reflection of candlelight in her eyes. Savannah had the most incredible eyes. They tried to be brown, but somehow managed to be blue near the pupil. Her face was on the square side, but that just made her full lips seem invitingly pouty.

Like most doctoral candidates he'd met, she had a penchant for wearing casual clothing. Only, she wore *tight* casual clothing. He knew it was the style. He also knew that when he returned to the kitchen, he'd have to pretend not to notice that her shape-hugging sweater fell just shy of the waistband of her jeans. He couldn't notice that she worked out enough to have a perfectly toned midriff, or that her belly button was pierced with a small gold ring.

Hell, he had to pretend that Savannah wasn't his ideal woman. Or that he thought of her often. *Too often.* It could jeopardize his professional integrity, something he had *never* done.

"What are you doing in there?" Savannah called. "Going through my panty drawer? Isn't that illegal?"

Seth put on his game face and returned to the main room. "It isn't illegal if I have your permission," he offered with a wicked smile.

"Dream on," she said with a laugh.

"Stay still until I tell you to move," Seth instructed. He bent next to her leg with the box top in his hand. Because she was so petite, he found himself eye-level with her bared skin. She smelled clean, fresh. He would only have to turn his head a fraction of an inch and his lips would be against the gentle curve of her waist.

"You should have warned me that this was going to be a long-term rescue effort," Savannah teased.

Seth put his libido in his back pocket and managed to trap the mouse inside the closed box. He smiled when he saw how frightened she was, even with the little thing safely inside the box.

"Now what?" he asked.

"Free him," Savannah insisted with conviction.

Seth sighed. "I know you're new to Jasper, so you must not know that this little guy came in here to keep from freezing to death outside."

The way she wrinkled her nose was adorable. It was just another of her quirks that he tucked away in his mind.

"What do I do, then?"

"You could get a cage and some feed and…"

"I don't do roommates, Sheriff," she said. "Especially furry ones that aren't house-trained and eat trash."

No roommates? He added that to his list. "I'll take care of it," he offered.

Her expression brightened just as the reflection of sunlight filtered inside, painting her shoulder-length brunette hair with auburn highlights.

"You're going to take care of it?" Savannah fairly gasped. "As in, a favor?"

Seth shrugged. "Sure. I'll run him out to the

Bronco for now so we can talk, and take him to the Lucky 7 on my way back to the office."

"You're taking him to your ranch? As a pet for Kevin?"

Seth blinked and Savannah blushed.

He allowed his mouth to curve into a slow grin. "Been checking up on me Miss Wyatt?"

Her lips pursed momentarily. "No," she insisted firmly. "Working part-time at Olive's Attic, I meet people. People tend to gossip about the richest family in town. By the way, how is Callie feeling?"

"Fine," Seth answered, hiding his disappointment. He wished she would show half the interest in him that she did on his brother Sam and Sam's expectant wife, Callie. Even before the first murder, he'd felt as if he were invisible to Savannah. He didn't like that feeling. Not at all.

"She'll tell you she feels like a whale, but I think pregnancy agrees with her."

He watched as something flashed in Savannah's kaleidoscope eyes. It wasn't long enough for him to get a read, so he had nothing to add to his list but a suspicion that babies, pregnancies, family—something along those lines—made her react, even if she was a master at hiding most of her reactions. Maybe today, with the new development, her facade would crumble.

After Seth had taken the mouse out to his car, he returned, walking in without knocking. That didn't seem to bother Savannah. She was standing in the living area, between a sofa covered with various warm throws and a coffee table made out of what looked like a portion of a wooden feed trough with a custom-cut glass top. When he took a second to glance around, he realized her place was homey in a funky, New Yorkish way. She had the usual stuff, living room, dining room and kitchen furnishings. But it was what she didn't have that tweaked his imagination. No photographs, nothing really personal in view. It was as if she hadn't existed until this cabin, but he knew that wasn't possible. He'd checked. Savannah was a transfer doctoral candidate from the University of Maryland. The dean of students at Montana West had verified all her paperwork and transfer credits.

"Should I make coffee?"

"Should you?" Seth countered.

She stiffened, "I was offering."

Seth smiled. "No, an offer is, 'May I make you some coffee?'"

Reluctantly, she smiled, as well. "Fine. *May* I make some coffee?"

"Please."

As she took down a grinder and retrieved a bag of whole beans, she asked, "Are you the resident grammar fairy? If so, you're welcome to critique my thesis. *If* I ever get it finished."

"I'm not a grammar anything. My momma just

insisted that all her boys be polite, especially to women." He let that sink in for a minute, then said, "Your thesis is on forensic psychology, right?"

Savannah turned and gave him a cool smile. "I keep forgetting that after Richard was killed, you investigated every aspect of my life."

"It's my job," Seth said somberly.

"If you're not here to arrest me for Richard's murder, would you kindly take an ad out in the town paper proclaiming my innocence? I've found Jasper a little slow to warm to outsiders, and labeling me a murder suspect isn't helping."

"I'm not here about Richard's murder."

That got Savannah's attention. "Since I didn't call 911 about the mouse, what brings you out this way?"

"Harvey Whitlock."

He watched and saw only a trace of boredom in her expression at the mention of his name.

"Sells real estate and is big on punctuality," Savannah supplied easily. "I was supposed to meet him at nine and I believe I was about ten minutes late because I was helping a customer at Olive's."

"Where did you meet him?"

"At the Mountainview Inn. Why?" Suspicion and trepidation had crept into her voice.

"Your idea?"

"No," she answered, less open than before. "Olive Baumgartner set it up as a blind date. She can't stand the fact that—her words—I'm 'on the ugly side of thirty and don't have any marriage prospects.'"

Seth smiled. Olive had arranged a date or two for nearly every single person of marriageable age in Jasper. Everyone except her precious Junior. Apparently she had no intention of letting go of her son. Not since Junior became the man of the house at the age of thirteen when Frederick, Sr. died in a hunting accident.

"So, your date with Harvey was just like your date with Richard?"

"Yes. Are you the dating police?" she asked with slight amusement. "If only you knew how ludicrous that was. You think I killed Richard so now you're going to keep track of all my dates?"

"Something like that," Seth answered.

"I'll save you some time. Harvey and I had dinner. He had the beef, I had the salmon. He had two drinks, I had a club soda and a cup of decaf."

"What did the two of you talk about?"

She rolled her eyes and a mischievous little grin curved her inviting lips. "Whether we should have sex right there in the restaurant, or go back to his place."

Seth felt his jaw clench. "What did you decide?"

"Neither. I was making a joke," she said, laughingly.

He felt the sound of her laughter deep in the pit of his stomach.

"We talked a lot about real estate. Harvey thinks I should buy rather than rent for the tax advantages. If I give him copies of my financial records, he will see about getting me qualified for that modest, gray clapboard house out on 141."

"That's a nice property. It comes with a dozen or so acres."

"Well, I'm really not into buying homes right now and I told Harvey that."

"What happened afterward?"

Savannah raked her hair out of her eyes as the gourmet coffeepot sputtered, then went silent. "At first, Harvey wanted to take me out to the property. You know, do a little hard sell?"

"At night?" Seth asked.

She handed him a cup of coffee and offered him cream and sugar, which he declined.

"That was my reaction. I still haven't acclimated to the Montana cold."

"So what did you do?"

Savannah gave him a wary glance. "I already told you I was joking about the sex. Nothing else happened."

"You said goodbye at the restaurant?"

"Yes—well, sort of."

"What is 'sort of'?" Seth asked, hoping beyond hope she wouldn't say it.

"We started out toward the parking lot when Harvey insisted we go down to the little bridge behind the inn to see the stream reflect the moonlight. I figured he was trying to be romantic."

"Was it?"

"*Not!* After about five minutes of saying hello to those idiots who jog that path in any weather, at all hours of the day and night, I left Harvey to enjoy the moonlight and the health freaks on his own."

"Did you see anyone in the parking lot? Did anyone see you leave? Maybe say goodbye?"

"Remember, I'm not very popular, but I don't think so. Why?"

Seth met and held her gaze. "Because Harvey Whitlock is dead."

He watched as Savannah's jaw dropped. Unsteadily, she balanced back on her hands against the countertop. "This *is not* possible. You can't seriously be telling me that I've had two blind dates in two weeks and they both died afterward."

"Kind of. The problem is, I can't find any evidence or witnesses that these men died *after* being with you."

Savannah gasped. "You can't think I killed two virtual strangers! I would have to be some sort of sicko Black Widow type!"

Seth took in a breath and let it out slowly.

"Are you?"

## Chapter Two

Main Street in Jasper had remained virtually un-
changed since it sprang up around the 1860s, twenty
years prior to Montana gaining statehood. Savannah
pulled into a parking spot on the street in the middle
of the block. Four expertly restored buildings stood
side by side in the shadows of the Rockies. Were it
not for the meters and one neon sign, she would
have felt very much as if she was stepping back in
time.

Once she exited her car, Savannah was careful not
to go in the direction of the newest building on the
block. Well, new was a bit of an exaggeration, she
mused as cold, clean air filled her lungs. The

sheriff's office had been built around the turn of the century, so the brick and barred-window building lacked the Victorian charm of the other homes-turned-businesses. She'd avoided him for two weeks, and she was content to keep it that way.

The moment she entered the shop, she was assailed with the strong aroma of homemade candles and heavily scented sachets. A bell tolled when she closed the door. "Olive?" she called out as she took off her heavy coat and hung it on the coatrack—which, like everything else in the shop, was for sale.

"Be down in a little bit! Junior and I are having a late lunch," Olive called from the second story.

Olive's Attic was exactly as the name implied. It was a cramped space filled with everything from locally dug arrowheads to tailored vintage clothing. And Savannah knew clothing.

She went over to one of the forms to examine a dress Olive had added to the inventory. Savannah read the designer tag from the twenties sewn into the garment, then read the ridiculously low price and knew her paycheck for the week was shot.

For Savannah, Olive's was like a small treasure trove. People from Jasper and the surrounding communities brought things to Olive on consignment, usually after a death in the family. Savannah smiled, thinking to herself that instead of calling Montana Big Sky Country, they should call it the Land of the Mothballs. It seemed as if no one ever threw out anything. They just left things in mothballs until ritualistically surrendering them to Olive for sale.

If Savannah had had the money to buy all the clothing in the store, she could run back to the Lower East Side with it and make a fortune.

*If.*

That word sent her into a temporary funk. Returning to her other life wasn't an option. Not if she wanted to stay alive.

Savannah was in the process of stripping the dress form when the bell tolled. She turned, smiling.

Smiling back at her was Sheriff Landry. Lord, she hated the way her pulse increased whenever she set eyes on the man! He walked toward her in a slow, easy swagger that conveyed confidence. His dark eyes were expressionless, but it didn't matter. His smile alone was gift enough.

"Is that for another date?" Seth asked, indicating the hand-beaded dress draped over her arm.

She met his gaze and ignored the allure of his cologne. "Maybe."

"Then I'll alert the coroner."

She gave him a smart-ass smile. "You do that."

Seth's demeanor remained annoyingly casual. "We need to talk."

"I'm working," she said, then began to tidy up a tray of assorted buttons.

"I'm sure Olive won't mind."

"Won't mind what?" Olive said as she carefully

descended the stairs. Today she was limping on her right leg and leaning on her son for support.

Yesterday, Savannah would have sworn it was the other leg. But she'd grown used to Olive's many ailments. She was basically a sweet woman, she just seemed to thrive on whatever happened to be her pain *du jour.* Olive spent almost as much time in the doctor's office as she did at the shop.

Seth tipped his hat to Olive and greeted Junior warmly. As far as Savannah knew, Seth was the only other person in town who was kind to Junior. "I need to speak to Savannah for a little while. Is that all right with you, Miss Olive?"

Olive patted the perfect bluish-white chignon at the nape of her neck, still leaning on her son for support. "I feel a spout of the gout coming on," Olive replied. "I was just going to go over to see that brother of yours. You have no idea how painful the gout can be." She squeezed her son's hand. "You kids should enjoy yourselves when you're young. Being old is such a trial."

Seth went over and assisted Junior in guiding his mother onto the rocker near the register. "How about if I get Chance to come to you?" he suggested. "That way you'll be spared the discomfort of walking down to his office."

Olive's green eyes brightened. Savannah wasn't sure whether it was from the attention she was getting from both men, or if she just relished the idea of a house call.

"May I use the phone?" Seth asked, his tone full of real or imagined sympathy.

"Yes. I'm in such pain, you know. The sooner he can get here the better."

"Then I can take Savannah with me?"

"What for?" Junior asked, meekly.

Seth slapped him reassuringly on the back. "Just a few questions and loose ends. Nothing earth-shattering."

Olive began to fan her face. "Seth Landry, don't you dare accuse poor Savannah of killing those men. You ought to be out looking for one of those predator killers I've seen on the TV."

"Yes, ma'am," Seth replied. "Give me a minute to call Chance."

While Seth was on the phone, Junior ventured in Savannah's direction. "You don't have to go with him," he half whispered. Junior was a very smart man in spite of his submissive personality. Savannah knew better than to insult his intelligence.

"He's harmless," Savannah insisted. "I've got nothing to be worried about. I didn't do anything."

"I know," Junior said with unusual force. "But when you're alone with him, you don't know what will happen. If you get into a jam, call me and I'll send a lawyer right over to the sheriff's office for you, okay?"

Savannah nodded and gave his forearm a gentle squeeze as she smiled up at her friend. "It will probably take less than a half hour," she promised him. "Can you take time away from your accounting work to help your mom?"

Junior's eyes were downcast again. "Of course. I always take care of Mother."

Savannah's heart tugged when she heard the devotion in the man's voice. So maybe some of the people in town thought mother and son were *too* close, but Savannah admired and even envied their bond.

"Chance and Val will be here asap," Seth announced after hanging up the phone.

"That brother of yours is wonderful," Olive fairly purred. "All of you Landrys are good boys, in spite of that unpleasantness with Clayton."

For the first time, Savannah saw Seth's happy facade slip. The devil-may-care look in his big, dark eyes was momentarily replaced by intense pain. The only gossip she had garnered about Clayton was that he was in prison. It had to be tough to be the town sheriff and have a criminal for a brother.

"We're still in the appeal process," Seth said. "The next hearing is set for spring."

Olive reached out withered hands to Seth. "You know we're all pulling for him."

"Thanks, Miss Olive."

Once again the bell tolled. "Hello, Dr. Landry. Miss Greene," Savannah greeted.

Chance gave her a wink and said, "Chance, please."

"Ditto here. I prefer Val," Chance's nurse said.

There was no doubt in Savannah's mind that the good Lord had smiled upon the Landry men. Chance was almost as attractive as his brother. His black hair was cut short and there were a few gray hairs at his temple. He also had the same sexy half smile as Seth.

*Sexy?* her little voice queried. I cannot find Seth sexy! *That* is against the rules.

"Ready?" Seth inquired.

Savannah simply nodded, afraid she might blurt out just exactly what she was ready for. And it wasn't another interrogation. She placed the beaded dress behind the counter and explained to Olive she was going to purchase it when she returned.

As she came around from behind the counter, Seth took her coat off the rack and held it out for her. The simple way he guided her arms inside the garment was the closest thing she'd come to foreplay in ages. She was aware of everything. The heat emanating from his large body. And the warmth generated by the feel of his fingertip brushing her neck as he gently pulled her hair free.

The even sound of his breathing was embarrassing. Mainly because hers was coming in shallow, hurried gulps. Maybe Junior was right. Maybe Seth could convince her of anything in an hour's time. If she didn't get her hormones in check, it would take him less than a minute to be able to convince her to have sex with him.

Luckily, as soon as they were outside the cold air slapped her in the face and brought her sense of reason back. It didn't matter if Seth was attractive and sexy. Montana was temporary. Hence, anything that started between them would have to be temporary by definition, and Savannah did not do temporary.

The snow piled near the curb was black and ugly. Nothing like the pristine, white-capped mountains she could see from her cabin. Lord, but she had hated that cabin when she first set eyes on it. Now, however, she had made it feel more like home, mostly with odds and ends she had picked up at the shop.

"You don't have to look so uncomfortable," Seth commented when they reached his office. "I don't use the bright lights and Taser on women."

"Gee, that's good to know."

He led her past his gawking deputy. J.D. was still young enough to be unable to keep his reaction to a beautiful woman in check. After feeling the softness of the skin at the nape of Savannah's neck, Seth had some serious doubts about his own abilities.

He offered her the chair across from his cluttered desk. Somehow, having a desk littered with pending DUI and poaching complaints between them made

Seth feel a little more comfortable. A little more like a professional.

Apparently following his lead, Savannah pulled off her coat and left it on the chair. If she was the least bit concerned, it didn't show on her face. Or in those incredible eyes of hers. Beneath the fluorescent light of his office, they appeared more brown than blue. Yet just a second earlier, out in the glare of the afternoon sun, he would have sworn they were more blue.

"Coffee?" he asked.

She shook her head.

"Tea, soda?"

"Nothing, thanks."

Seth pushed some papers around on his desk, trying to see if his stall tactic made her nervous. It didn't. He continued to shuffle things around. "So, why did you pick forensic psychology?"

"To understand why people commit crimes," was her easy answer.

He lifted his eyes to hers and suggested, "Because they're criminals?"

That elicited a smile from her. "Granted. But don't you want to know the motives of the people you arrest?"

He shrugged. "Motive isn't necessary for prosecution."

She leaned forward to the edge of the desk.

*Bad move,* he decided. That simple action made

the pale pink sweater further outline her delicious body. The delicious body he wasn't supposed to be noticing.

"Don't you feel better, though, when you know why a crime was committed?"

Reluctantly, he nodded. "I suppose."

"Someday, law enforcement officers like you will be able to call on people like me to help you solve crimes by understanding the criminal."

*If I call you, it won't be to discuss a criminal.* "What got you interested in the psychology of crime?"

Seth noticed that she averted her gaze. He added that to his list.

"Because I think people sometimes get involved in crimes without even knowing it. They aren't criminals, but our current system treats them as such."

Seth stroked his chin and felt his annoyance level rise. "Nice answer. Did you get that from town gossip about Clayton? Did you think if you sounded the trumpets in defense of my brother I'd forget that you're the prime suspect in two murders?"

Savannah's reaction was quick and harsh. "I don't know squat about your brother other than he's in prison. I was speaking in the abstract."

"It didn't sound abstract," Seth retorted. Then his mind went in a completely different direction. "Or, are you setting me up for a self-defense plea?"

"Self-defense?"

"Fowler and Whitlock wouldn't take no for an answer, so you had no choice but to shoot them?"

Raw fury shone in her eyes. "I didn't shoot anybody! I passed your paraffin tests after both shootings, remember?"

"That could just mean you wore gloves."

Savannah stood and grabbed her coat, ramming her arms into the sleeves. "In case you haven't noticed, I don't wear gloves. And if this is your idea of a talk to clear a few things up, you and I have completely different definitions of the word *talk*. Goodbye, Sheriff."

"Wait!"

She stilled at his commanding tone, but her angry eyes never left his face.

"Are you going to arrest me?"

"No."

"Then I have every right to leave."

"True, but I'd like to ask you two questions before you do."

He could tell her acquiescence was only half-hearted. "Fine. Two questions."

"Do the numbers 9-1-2 mean anything to you?"

"No."

"Are you sure?"

She glared at him. "Is that your second question?"

Seth felt the string of his patience pull taut. "No,

my second question is…why is there no trace of any Savannah Wyatt prior to your records from the University of Maryland?"

# Chapter Three

"What do you mean, no trace?" Savannah challenged.

To Seth's eyes, her body language was screaming retreat. He kept his gaze level. "I mean your social security number had no activity until six years ago. You have no credit history, never attempted to buy a home or an apartment. Nothing. Nada."

"I didn't work before college, and—" she paused and took in a long breath "—and I lived with my family, so I had no reason to use my social security card."

"Let me see it."

"What?" Savannah asked. He could almost smell her panic.

"I'd like to see your social security card," he repeated evenly.

"I—it's back at the cabin."

Seth nodded. "Okay." He reached for the telephone. "Then I'll just call your family to verify your story."

"You can't!" Savannah fairly yelled.

Seth lifted one dark brow questioningly. "You do have parents I can call, right?"

He saw sadness glaze her beautiful eyes and realized his little game might backfire.

"They passed away," she said softly. "Six years ago."

Seth felt like every kind of fool. "I'm sorry."

She shrugged. "You get used to not having them around—eventually."

"I know."

Savannah looked at him through her feathery brown lashes. "You lost your parents, too?"

He gave a weak smile. "Sort of, I lost mine *literally*."

"Excuse me?"

Seth drummed his thumbs against his desktop. "My mother ran off with another man."

"How terrible."

"Then my thickheaded father went after her. That was ten years ago. Haven't seen or heard from either of them since."

"That's incredible," Savannah said in a near

whisper. "It must have been hard on you. But at least you had your brothers."

Seth rubbed his face. "We all handled it differently. But we handled it, except for Shane. He's the baby of the family. Runs the day-to-day at Lucky 7, when he isn't trying in vain to impress Taylor Reese," Seth said with a quick smile. "He wandered back into town about a year ago and took over."

"Where was he wandering?"

"You have to understand, Shane and the old man didn't get along very well. They had a huge blowout when Pop decided he was going to go out and bring back what was his—meaning my mother—Shane was only eighteen at the time and I guess he had to conduct his own search or something."

"What about you?" Savannah asked. "Why can't you find them? You're a sheriff."

"They don't want to be found," Seth said with conviction. "I spent two years contacting every jurisdiction in the country. If people want to disappear, they can."

Savannah suddenly sat back down in the chair and offered her rapt attention. "Do you really think so? Do you really think a person *can't* be found?"

Seth added this apparent interest in missing persons to his list. "Sure. If they're careful."

"Yes, I guess a person would have to be very careful not to be found," she mused, her expression faraway. Suddenly, she returned to the here and now and asked, "Are we finished?"

"For now," Seth said. "I'll be out to your place tonight to take a look at that social security card."

"My place?" she repeated, apparently stunned. "I'll just bring it to you tomorrow."

"No," he said more forcefully, "I'll come to you."

Seth moved to the window to watch Savannah walk back to Olive's. He also watched as she stopped to use the pay phone in front of the post office. He stood in the shadows of the venetian blinds as she spent several animated minutes on the phone. Next, he watched as she put several more coins in the telephone, covered the mouthpiece, appeared to listen for a second, then hang up. She was one incredibly secretive, strange, but very beautiful woman.

Seth moved back to his desk and called the phone company to ask for the LUDs for the pay phone Savannah had just used. If she was going to be secretive, he was going to have to work that much harder to prove—

*Prove what?* he asked himself. The answer was simple and immediate. To prove she wasn't a killer. Because that's what he wanted. *She* was what he wanted.

"NO WAY!" Savannah insisted firmly just after her return to the shop.

"Bill Grayson is an old friend of Junior's. They went to school together!" Olive argued.

"Olive, the last two times you've set me up on a date, the men have become corpses."

"Oh, pooh," Olive dismissed with a wave of her gnarled hand. "I know you didn't kill them."

"If Bill Grayson is a family friend, then why don't you set him up with someone else?"

"Like who?"

"Taylor Reese," Savannah suggested. "I've had coffee with her at the university. She's nice, attractive—"

"Way too young," Olive said after considering it. "The Landry's housekeeper is too immature, too flighty. Bill is over forty. Besides, all I'm asking you to do is have dinner with him at the inn."

"No."

"Savannah?" Olive pleaded, "Please? How about if I send Junior along, too? He can sit at the bar and watch over the two of you? You won't have to leave the inn. You just have a nice dinner in plain view of all the patrons. Junior will be there to make sure nothing happens to Bill or you."

*To me?* A shiver danced along her spine. Jasper was supposed to be a safe haven. *Right?* Savannah closed her eyes. She knew her determination was slipping away. Olive and Junior were the closest thing she had to family.

She looked sternly at the shop owner. "First, you have to tell Bill about my last two dates."

"Already did that," Olive returned with a smile. "Once I told him what a beauty you were, he didn't seem to mind."

"Second, Junior has to stay at the bar the whole time. *And* he has to walk me to my car afterward."

"Done."

Savannah blew out a breath. "What time?"

"Eight."

Savannah checked her watch. She had less than two hours to drive to her cabin, change and be at the inn on time.

As if sensing her calculations, Olive said, "Run along. And wear your new dress," she added, handing Savannah the neatly wrapped beaded dress.

Nearly an hour later as she entered her cabin, Savannah asked, "What are the chances of it happening again? None? Less than none?"

She stripped off her clothes for a shower, then got ready faster than a trunk-show model. The pale ivory color of the dress complimented her olive-tinged skin. And the drop waist meant she could eat her fill and not have to worry about it showing.

Grabbing a pair of heels from her closet, she stuffed them into a bag. Then she began to switch items from her leather bag to a smaller evening bag. That's when she came across the social security card and cursed.

It was completely unsullied and looked as if it had never seen the light of day. Quickly, Savannah crumpled it, then set a teapot on the stove to further steam-age the card. She even went so far as to smudge some ink on it. *That should satisfy the handsome Sheriff Landry.*

"Stop thinking of him as handsome," she chided as she pulled on her boots. "Stop thinking of him period."

Not even daring to use the word *date,* she scribbled a note to Seth explaining that she had other plans, then tacked the card to the front door before she headed back toward Jasper.

Junior greeted her in the Mountainview Inn's parking lot. He was standing with an attractive man dressed in a Prada suit. Savannah's expectations rose a notch.

"Savannah, this is Bill Grayson." Junior introduced them.

She smiled as she extended her free hand. "Nice to meet you, Mr. Grayson."

"Bill," he fairly cooed.

*I don't like cooers,* Savannah thought. *They're almost as bad as grovelers.* But, hey, she was having dinner with him, not children.

Savannah went into the ladies' room and switched her snow boots for her pumps. As was the custom, she left her boots on the tile floor inside the bathroom to dry during her meal.

When she emerged, Bill was seated at a table near the large window of the A-frame building. In her peripheral vision, she spotted Junior at the bar, watching her reflection in the glass behind the counter.

"I haven't been back here in almost a year," Bill said as he pulled out her chair. "But it isn't like Jasper ever changes."

"It's pretty once you get used to it," Savannah offered.

Bill's blue eyes roamed freely over Savannah, in spite of her silent rebuke of crossing her arms in front of her chest.

"So, what brings you back to town?" Savannah asked after they had ordered drinks.

"Diamonds and rubies."

She studied Bill's expression and determined he was serious. "Real diamonds and rubies?"

He nodded as he took a sip of his beer. "My family made its money in gold mining. I didn't want to join the family business, so I branched out."

"Pretty expensive branch," Savannah commented as an elegant salad of field greens and raspberry vinaigrette was placed before her.

"I used a small portion of my family trust to start my own wholesale business."

"Why wholesale?" she asked. "Wouldn't a store have a higher profit margin?"

He offered her a smile full of perfectly capped

teeth at the very instant she noted a familiar silhouette reflected in the window behind Bill's perfectly coifed hair.

*Seth Landry. Damn!* she thought silently.

Bill was explaining something about his business, but Savannah was distracted as she watched Seth join Junior at the bar. Whatever he said to Junior made the shy man laugh.

She watched for a few more seconds as anger formed and grew in the pit of her stomach. Seth and Junior seemed to be having a fine old time. Surely Junior had told Seth what he was doing at the bar. So why hadn't Seth turned in her direction? Worse still, why did she want him to? The guy had her brain all twisted.

"…must be boring you," Bill commented, his cheeks stained a pale pink.

Savannah regrouped and gave him her very best smile. In a feline fashion, Savannah reached out and touched Bill's hand, then made breeze-soft circles on his palm. "Not at all," she assured him. "I was just distracted for an instant. Please, continue."

Bill's fit body seemed to swell inside his designer silk jacket as a result of her suddenly rapt attention. And Bill wasn't the only one to notice. In the reflection she could see that both Junior and Seth had swiveled on their bar stools and were openly watching them.

Bill, thankfully, was oblivious. He continued his

mostly one-sided conversation even after their entrées were served. "At first I was going to go the jewelry store route, but if you grow up in a small town, you either love it or hate it," he explained.

"I'll guess you hated it," Savannah said.

Bill nodded and then waved in the direction of the bar. To Savannah's utter mortification, Junior was leaving. Actually, the mortification was because, apparently, Seth was staying. Nothing like having the sheriff as your babysitter on a date.

"You're nice to Junior," Savannah opined with genuine admiration.

"He had it rough," Bill said. "He's always had that lisp and those glasses. The kids were cruel to him growing up, which was exactly what he didn't need. Especially after his dad died in a hunting accident when he was about thirteen."

Savannah remembered that there were no photographs of Olive's husband around. Perhaps losing someone she loved suddenly had been so painful, Olive preferred not to display them. "Children can be nasty to one another." She repressed her desire to recall some of the hateful things she and her siblings had said to one another over the years. All chances for her to apologize had ended six years ago.

"Don't look so depressed. Junior took most of it in stride and he always had Olive to rebuild his self-esteem."

"Still," Savannah commented, "it must have hurt to have every kid in town ragging on him."

"Not every kid," Bill corrected. "Seth made sure of that."

"Seth—as in Sheriff Seth?"

Bill nodded, but his mood seemed to sour. "The same Seth who is sitting over there watching us."

It was Savannah's turn to blush. "I think he thinks he's doing his job."

Bill snorted dismissively. "I had a couple of reservations about this evening, but now that I've met you, I can't believe for one minute that you're some sort of serial killer."

"Thanks. You're a minority, though."

"That's why I left town as soon as I could. The gossip mongering in this town makes Peyton Place seem like the friendliest community on earth."

They both laughed. Then Savannah asked, "Were you ever the subject of gossip?"

"Sure. When I was seventeen, the whole town knew I lost my virginity before I did."

Savannah laughed again. She was beginning to relax. Bill's sense of humor was a wonderful salve on her frazzled nerves. "I think you're exaggerating."

"A bit. But I got labeled as a—" he made quote signs with his fingers "—pillager of Jasper's crop of young women."

"Seventeen is pretty young."

Bill made a noncommittal move with his shoulders. "I got lucky all of two times when I lived here. The pillagers were the sainted Landry brothers. But no one dared disparage a Landry. Not in Jasper."

Based on his sudden frown, she realized Bill wasn't fond of their lookout. "I guess boys will be boys," Savannah quipped, hoping to lighten the tone of the conversation.

"They weren't boys, they were a herd," Bill countered with open hostility. "It wasn't like you could have a beef with one of them. If you made one Landry mad, they all showed up to dole out some attitude adjustment."

"I've met Sam and his wife. They seem awfully nice."

Bill downed the remainder of his drink. "I don't know why I'm complaining about them now. That was more than twenty years ago and they all seem to have settled down. At least, that's what my mother used to claim in her letters."

"Enough about Landrys," Savannah insisted. "Since there's no jewelry shop in Jasper, I'll assume you just stopped for the night for old times' sake?"

"For Angelica Seagal," Bill countered with a wide grin.

"Sorry, the name isn't familiar."

"Angelica designs jewelry. I supply the gemstones."

"So you have to come all the way here from... speaking of which, where is your home base?"

"Saint Paul. And if I didn't come here to haggle with Angelica, she'd find a way to hunt me down."

"Why?"

"Angelica and I go way back. She was my prom date, in fact."

"Seagal Signature Jewelry?" Savannah asked, suddenly putting the name together with the pricey jewelry sold in only the top jewelry stores. A Seagal Signature was the present-day equivalent of having a Louis Comfort Tiffany piece at the turn of the century.

"The very one."

"I had no idea Jasper had a genuine celebrity."

"Angelica is an artist," Bill said. "Which really only means she's a bit on the weird side. She has some live-in assistant. His name is Vincent."

"Vincent what?" Savannah queried. "Maybe I've met him."

"Just *Vincent*," Bill said with humor in his voice. "He looks a little bit like Lurch from *The Addams Family,* only with white hair."

"I think I've seen him walk past the shop to the post office. He is a tad on the creepy side," she admitted with a wicked grin.

"I believe Angelica thinks it's terribly artsy to have Vincent around. If nothing else, he's probably a good deterrent to anyone thinking of breaking into her studio."

"Where does she work?"

"The old assay office at the end of Main Street. But I wouldn't suggest visiting. Angelica is very private."

Savannah pushed away her nearly empty plate. "I wouldn't dream of disturbing a genius at work. But I would love to see some of her work up close—not behind the glass of a store window."

Bill finished his plate, as well. "I can't show you her work, but I can show you some sketches she sent me and the jewels I brought for them."

Savannah felt her eyes grow wide. "Really?"

"Sure," Bill said. "I've got them up in my room."

He must have registered her reaction to the notion of going to his room because he added, "I have no ulterior motive," he promised. "Although, if you're interested, I'm game," he teased.

"Sorry," Savannah said on a breath. "I've really enjoyed having dinner with you, but it stops there, okay?"

"No," he said as he stood, pulled several bills from his pocket and took her hand. "It stops right after I show you Angelica's sketches and the most incredible diamonds, rubies and emeralds anywhere on the face of God's great earth."

Savannah pretended to ignore the look of censure from Seth as she followed Bill to the guest room elevators.

Once they were inside the elevator compartment, Bill asked, "Am I poaching on Landry territory?"

"Heavens, no!" she insisted. "Seth's only interest in me is professional."

"The looks he's been giving you all night look more personal to me."

"He was probably just hoping I'd whip out a .22 and shoot you at the table so he could close his investigation."

"He'll figure out who did the other murders," Bill assured her as he guided her inside his suite. "Seth can be a pain, but he's pretty good at his job."

Savannah surveyed the room. There was a comfortable living room area with beautiful views of the moonlit mountains in the distance. She ran her hand along the edge of the leather sofa while Bill disappeared into the adjoining room, closing the door as he mumbled something about a safe. It was quiet in the room, save for the insulation. She could hear muffled voices and the sound of a car backfiring in the parking lot below.

Savannah checked her watch. Bill had been in the bedroom for almost ten minutes. *Maybe he's in the little gem sellers' room,* she thought. After another minute went by, Savannah called out to him.

Just as she did, there was a knock at the door. Savannah was still calling Bill's name when she opened the door to a scowling Seth.

A scowling Seth with his weapon drawn.

"What are you doing?"

"Where is he?" Seth barked.

"In the bedroom. He went in there about ten minutes ago to bring out some gems to show me."

Seth shoved her onto the sofa as he went to the door and kicked it in.

From her vantage point, Savannah could see Bill on the floor.

Blood trickled from a single hole in his forehead.

# Chapter Four

Ignoring Savannah's shocked expression, Seth raced out into the hall, crouched and ready to fire. Only problem was, there was no one in the long, deserted hallway.

It made no sense, he thought as he returned to Bill Grayson's suite and called the coroner and J.D. Savannah was as still as a painting.

He went over to where she sat on the couch, stark white and staring blankly into space. He took her hands in his. She was trembling.

"He was shot with a .22. Where's the gun, Savannah?"

His question brought her out of her fog. "The gun? I don't have a gun! I didn't shoot him."

Seth frowned deeply, trying to make sense of her proclamations of innocence and the conflicting facts.

The facts were he had received a call of shots fired at the inn and was inside the elevator in less than ten seconds after the call. It was maybe a total of thirty seconds before he kicked in the door to Grayson's bedroom. The room still smelled of gunpowder. Meaning the fatal shot had been fired within the last few moments. He checked his watch, noting the time was 9:33.

Though there was a second exit from the bedroom, Seth had already noted that it was bolted from the inside. Which meant the killer had to run past Savannah to make his quick escape. Or—

*Or she was the killer.*

"I have to search you and your bag," Seth explained.

Savannah's ire had begun to rise. She held her arms out to her sides and said, "Search away."

Seth had her turn so her back was to him. She felt him grab a handful of her vintage dress and pull it taut against her body. "You break it, you bought it," she snidely commented. "Those seams you're straining were sown when people like you were busy chasing Al Capone."

Using his nightstick, Seth ran it along her entire body. She should have been furious at the indignity of it, but for some reason, she wasn't. Maybe it was just that it had been too long since she'd had any close contact with a man. Savannah almost laughed aloud at that absurd thought. What she was inappropriately feeling had nothing to do with men in general. It had to do with *this* man. Mainly because she could hear the slight catch in his breath when he checked the more intimate areas of her body. She only hoped the reverse wasn't true. She didn't want to give him the satisfaction.

Dr. Hall, the coroner, and J.D. arrived then, moving into the adjoining bedroom on Seth's command. Dumping the contents of her purse on the coffee table, Seth found nothing of interest—except for a foil-wrapped condom. Savannah wanted the floor to open and swallow her as Seth gave her one of those "Big plans, eh?" looks.

"Better safe than sorry," she said, realizing it was a pretty lame comment. But it sounded better than *That thing's been in my purse for years and I'd forgotten about it until just now.* She was sure he wouldn't believe the truth.

"Stand up, please."

"Why?"

His expression was a mixture of frustration and restraint. "I have to cuff you."

"Cuff me?" she parroted, unbelieving. "But I didn't do anything!"

"I have to take you in for a paraffin test and another statement."

Savannah let out a deflating sigh. "Not again."

Seth met her exasperated gaze. "I don't have a

choice, Savannah. Unless you can explain how someone else managed to shoot Bill, then vanish."

J.D. entered the room. "That ain't all that vanished. The safe is open and there's nothing in it. We found an invoice in his briefcase. Said he had more than a million in gems on him."

Savannah felt the cold, hard handcuffs being snapped into place.

Dr. Hall emerged and said, "Judging by the body temperature and the air temperature measurements, this guy's only been dead for about ten minutes. Not even enough time for any lividity to begin."

"Let's go, Savannah."

She struggled against his hold. "Hasn't it occurred to any of you geniuses that Seth didn't find a gun *or* any jewels on me? He was here within minutes of the shot being fired. When did I have time to hide the murder weapon and the gems?"

"Good point," Seth said.

Savannah relaxed a bit.

"J.D., tear this room apart. The murder weapon and the gems must still be here."

Savannah called him a hateful name as he led her out of the suite and down through the gauntlet of gawkers to his Bronco. She hadn't killed Bill, but she would gladly have killed Seth in that instant.

HE WAS IMPRESSED. She hadn't shed a single tear. Savannah had taken the paraffin test, then asked permission to make a phone call. Seth guessed she had more class in her little finger than most folks had in their whole bodies. It had about killed him to send her downstairs to the matron, Mable. But the cavity search was necessary with a million bucks worth of gems missing.

Seth locked his hands behind his head and squeezed his weary eyes closed. Save for the lack of the weapon and other evidence, Savannah was the only logical suspect. *Then why do I feel like I'm putting together a jigsaw puzzle with one piece missing?*

"Uh, Sheriff?" J.D. hesitantly questioned from the doorway.

Seth let out a breath and rubbed the stubble on his chin. "What!"

J.D. jumped a bit at Seth's harsh tone.

"I mean," Seth began more amicably, "What do you have?"

"The matron didn't find any gems during the search. She suggested we take her to get an X ray in case she swallowed them. There was nothing at the hotel. We didn't find the suspect's fingerprints in the room. Just the dead guy and a partial thumbprint on the door."

"Which one?"

"The main door," J.D. answered.

"Great," Seth groused. "Who knows how long that's been there? Send it to the state police and ask them to run it."

"Yes, sir." J.D. turned to leave.

"And while you're at it, ask them when I can expect the background reports on Fowler and Whitlock. Ask them to start the drill on Bill Grayson, too. Maybe he didn't have a million dollars worth of gems, which would explain why we can't find them."

"Okay. You look tired," J.D. observed.

"Beat," Seth concurred. "But since I just awakened Judge Duckett for a search warrant for Savannah's home and workplace, my night isn't over yet." Seth slipped on his department-issue parka and started toward the door. He hesitated briefly at the top of the stairs leading to the cells below. He was secretly glad Mable hadn't found the gems.

Who was he kidding? He wasn't standing there thinking about gems. He was thinking about the necessary invasive procedure that had been done to Savannah. He was remembering the look of unbridled hate in her multicolored eyes when he was performing the paraffin test. For some reason, her hatred cut to the bone.

Just like the frigid January air that battered him as he walked the few steps to his Bronco. He'd have to drive an hour into Helena to get the warrant, then two hours to Savannah's cabin. He decided to stop at the Cowboy Café off Jasper Park to have Ruthie fill him a thermos of coffee. It was going to be a long night.

The parking lot was filled with pickups and semis. No matter what time of day you went in, the place smelled of bacon and coffee. He sauntered up to the chipped Formica counter, squeezing between two turquoise Naugahyde stools. One of the stool cushions was being held together with a worn, curled piece of duct tape.

Ruthie greeted him immediately. She was an attractive redhead, divorced, with a thirteen-year-old who was working real hard on finding his way into juvenile detention. It wasn't that Ruthie was a bad mother to Cal. Quite the opposite. It was just that Ruthie was forced to work nights to keep them in their modest mobile home, which meant Cal was basically without supervision. Too bad, too, since the kid was as smart as all hell. During his minor brushes with Seth, Cal had impressed him with his intelligence. Too bad he had a chip the size of Glacier National Park on his shoulder. Intelligence and bad attitude could be a deadly combination.

"Hi, there," Ruthie said, leaning half across the counter so that Seth could—had he wanted to—look directly down the front of her tight blue waitress's uniform. He smiled and passed on the opportunity yet again. Their relationship had ended more than two years ago. And he knew her flirtations were harmless, kind of her way of thanking him for keeping watch over Cal. Unfortunately, her actions fed the speculation of the town. Nearly everyone thought he was still involved with Ruthie. They wouldn't even listen to his explanation that they were just good friends.

"I need a thermos to go."

Ruthie's green eyes grew wide. "Is it true? Did the Black Widow strike again?"

"Haven't seen any black widows in these parts this time of year."

Ruthie pouted. "You know who I mean. That snooty woman who won't tell no one where she's from 'cept 'back East.'"

"If you're talking about Miss Wyatt, then I have no comment."

"What's that supposed to mean?" Ruthie demanded as she passed him a full thermos.

"It means I can't discuss an open investigation."

Ruthie smirked. "Then it's true! She killed old Billy Grayson for them jewels he was always bringing to Angelica. She's another snooty one, by the way."

"Thanks for the coffee," Seth said, tossing a few dollars on the counter. Ruthie made sure she had his attention as she slipped the bills not into the register, but into her lacy brassiere.

As he drove northwest in the blackness, Seth was perplexed. He always flirted with Ruthie. It was like a ritual. So why tonight had he found her so… so…brazen? *Because Savannah wouldn't bare her bosom for a dollar tip.* How in the hell had Savannah gotten under his skin like this? Cripe! She was a suspect, not a potential bride.

"Damn!" Seth spilled hot coffee on his hand at the mere thought of the word *bride*. Until just then, he didn't think the word was in his vocabulary. He loved women, all women. But never just one woman. *Especially* not the only woman currently sitting in one of his jail cells.

IT WAS NEARLY three in the morning when Seth arrived at Savannah's cabin. Using the keys from the evidence bag collected at the Mountainview Inn, he let himself inside.

Almost instantly he was assaulted with all kinds of feminine scents. He could make out jasmine, gardenia and lilac. He realized the odors were from the scented candles that she had everywhere. But there was a subtler scent under all the florals. It was the faint shadow of her perfume.

*I'm here to search, not get aroused,* he warned himself.

By the light of the half-moon, Seth went over to a floor lamp and pulled on the fringed tassel to turn it on. It was truly an eclectic room.

The red sofa was at an angle, a corner cabinet placed behind it. The coffee table sat on some faux fur rug and he found a footstool covered in the same faux fur. There was a white-and-green chair by the mason fireplace. There must have been fifty pillows of assorted sizes and shapes on the furniture and tossed around the room. She also had an odd collection of old hatboxes mixed with some large wooden boxes off in one corner. He decided to start there.

As he reached for the first hatbox, he noticed the walls. They were painted a muted green, and someone—Savannah was his guess—had taken the time to stencil a border of red-and-white flowers with green vines all around the room. Above the floor lamp illuminating the room, he discovered that she had stenciled a birdcage, complete with bird. It was so real, he half expected it to break into song at any moment.

Though Seth had managed to keep it out of the papers, the killer had taken trophies from each victim. According to Fowler's family, he always wore a silver pendant around his neck. Because of his work with his church, he had a Saint Barnabas medal on his person at all times. Except when his body had been fished from the freezing waters of Brock Creek behind the Mountainview Inn.

Bill Grayson's jewels were missing—another trophy taken. He was still waiting on information about Harvey Whitlock from the state police.

Serial killers were known for taking trophies. According to criminal profilers, they used the trophies to allow themselves to relive each murder. They usually kept the items close at hand—either at home or at work.

If Savannah was a serial killer, then he should find something from the earlier two murders here or at Olive's Attic.

The hatboxes and wooden crates he had believed to be simple decorations for her diverse tastes turned out to be little treasure troves.

After slipping on a pair of latex gloves, Seth started to inventory his findings. The hatboxes were filled with photographs. It was easy for him to find Savannah in the pictures. She'd been born with those incredible eyes. He was looking at a time capsule of her life. Savannah alone, then as the years passed, three small boys were added to the pictures of family vacations and holidays. All the important things were covered—birthdays, holidays, etc. Unfortunately, other than vacations to easily distinguishable locations, none of the photographs gave him a definite impression on where she had grown up. All he could tell was that she was from some East Coast state with four seasons. Or, it could mean that she and her family simply vacationed often.

Speaking of family, Savannah had given him the impression that she was an orphaned only child. As he took a fast-forward look through her past, it was plainly obvious that the three boys were her younger brothers. Their resemblance to one another ruled out cousins or other versions of relatives. He'd know those blue-brown eyes anywhere.

In the bottom of the second hatbox, he found a

graduation photograph. Savannah's entire family surrounded the youngest brother, who was dressed in cap, gown and acne. In the background, he could just make out a partial name of the high school. It appeared to be an urban setting. *If* she was from Maryland as she claimed, it shouldn't be too hard for him to fax the photograph to the Maryland State Police for identification. Seth tagged and bagged the picture.

Dawn was threatening when Seth reached for the first wooden crate. It was at that moment that he heard a key being inserted into the front door.

Kneeling down, Seth unholstered his weapon, held it in a two-handed grip, and then stopped breathing as he trained the muzzle on the slowly opening door.

"Good gracious, Seth Landry!" Olive screeched. "Put that gun down before you give me a heart attack!"

He holstered his gun as Junior dutifully followed his mother into the cabin, carrying a basket. Seth could smell freshly baked bread along with Olive's vapor trail of perfume.

"I can't believe you left her in jail all night," Junior said in an angry tone Seth had never heard during their nearly forty years of acquaintance. "You know she isn't a killer. *How* can you do this?"

"It's my job," Seth explained, irritated by their intrusion. Hell, he was just irritated period. "I don't mean to be rude, Olive, but I need to finish my work here and I can't have you and Junior traipsing through the place like you own it."

"I do own it," Olive reminded him.

"Sorry, I forgot. But I must insist that you leave now. I'll be by the shop later today for a look around."

"The shop?" Junior said, his voice high-pitched with apparent indignation. "What for?"

Seth met his eyes, which were magnified to an unnatural size by his thick, black-rimmed glasses. "I have a warrant to search Savannah's work area as well as her home."

Olive planted her hands on her ample hips and glared at Seth. "If you think I'm going to let you tear my shop apart on some wild-goose chase, you have another think coming. And if you get within ten feet of my bedroom, I'll get the shotgun and fill your backside with buckshot!"

"Unless Savannah has access to your upstairs apartment, I'll only be searching the first floor."

Olive snorted with obvious disgust.

"Are you going to leave her in jail while you do all this?" Junior asked.

Seth shrugged, knowing that he could hold her for twenty-four hours before pressing charges or cutting her loose.

Olive grabbed the basket from Junior and virtually slammed it into Seth's stomach. "I made some bread and put in some of my strawberry preserves. You take this to Savannah in that awful jail so she can have some proper food or I won't allow you to search my shop."

Seth nodded. "I'll see that she gets it."

"You know you're all wrong about her," Junior said, subdued. "We watched them together until you made me leave."

"That's true!" Olive piped in. "If you would have let Junior stay and keep an eye on them, none of this would have happened. I promised Savannah that Junior would keep her in his sight the entire night. You had no business sending him home at nine o'clock."

"That would have been difficult after Bill took her up to his suite."

Redness spread from Junior's thick neck to his face. "*I* would have gone up with them."

"Maybe Bill had other ideas," Seth remarked as delicately as possible.

Junior shook his head furiously. "Bill and I had a talk in his suite before Savannah arrived. I told him she wasn't that kind of woman, so he shouldn't even try."

"She did go to his room willingly," Seth pointed out. "We have no way of knowing why they went to his room." Seth's gut knotted when he stated the obvious.

Junior's face was now a burning red. "I'm sure it was perfectly innocent. Bill gave me his word."

Seth didn't want to argue the point. He wondered if Junior had any notion of the kind of ideas a man could get alone in a hotel room with Savannah. Probably not, since he was his mother's eunuch. In fact, Seth couldn't recall Junior having more than a dozen dates in recent history. None at all since Savannah had come to town.

The light dawned sometime after Olive and Junior had marched haughtily out of the cabin. The normally meek Junior had displayed a lot of emotion. Seth guessed that Junior had a major crush on Savannah. Poor guy. It must have felt pretty masochistic when mommy had assigned him the chore of watching Savannah have dinner with one of his friends.

Hell, Seth hadn't exactly enjoyed watching the sensual way she had touched Bill's hand. He could still hear the sound of her laughter, still see the way her dress complimented her figure. He wondered if she knew that candlelight made her eyes look even more exotic.

He wondered why he was recalling personal details when he was supposed to be conducting a search. "Lack of sleep," he grumbled as he moved into the bedroom.

Her bed was at an angle and unmade. He could see the faint imprint of her head on the pillow. That required further investigation. He lifted the pillow from the bed and drank in the smell of her. A sudden vision of Savannah in his bed with her dark hair fanned out framing her face caused the expected physical reaction.

"Geez, Junior has a crush and I'm teetering on the border of obsession. What is it about her?" he asked with a healthy dose of self-loathing.

Seth went through her closet and was amazed by the amount of her clothing. Some had labels, but most didn't, which struck him as odd. He couldn't even find a place where the labels had been removed.

He checked all thirty-one pairs of her shoes as possible hiding places. Then he went to her dresser. The top three drawers contained undergarments and neatly folded sweaters.

The bottom drawer was another matter. It was full, but not with clothing.

## Chapter Five

Seth returned to his office after a fruitless search of Savannah's home and Olive's Attic to find Savannah, the matron and some guy who looked as if he just stepped out of the Conservative-of-the-Month calendar.

The matron left almost instantly, but Seth barely noticed. He was too intent on studying the expression on Savannah's pretty face.

As he placed the picnic basket on his desk, he realized she looked gaunt and pale. He'd seen that kind of look before. It was the same expression he encountered whenever he had the grim job of ringing a doorbell in the middle of the night to tell some unprepared parents that their child had died in a car crash.

That was definitely what he read in Savannah's expression and it twisted a knot in his gut to see her like that.

The suit and tie rose and offered his hand. "Peter White," he said amicably.

Seth returned the greeting, then walked around to the opposite side of the desk. Savannah wouldn't even meet his gaze.

"What can I do for you, Mr. White?" he inquired.

Lifting a chrome briefcase into his lap, he flipped open the latches and retrieved several documents stapled inside the recognizable blue title pages.

Even running on no sleep, Seth knew instantly that this White guy was Savannah's lawyer. Interesting part was, he'd never seen nor heard of a lawyer named Peter White in any of the surrounding towns or counties.

"This," Peter began as he handed Seth the first of three sets of papers, "is a Show Cause order from the Federal District Court. It gives you until noon today to charge Miss Wyatt."

*Federal court?* Seth thought through the fog of his sleep-deprived brain. Why would the Feds be interested in a murder investigation in a town with a population of less than two thousand?

"And this," Peter continued, "is an order from

the Federal Bench placing Miss Wyatt in my custody until you respond to the Show Cause order."

"Why do you want her?" Seth asked.

"That's irrelevant at this time, Sheriff. And lastly, I have an order requiring you to turn over copies of any and all evidence related to the murders."

"Irrelevant my ass!" Seth snapped. "You can eat your court orders until you tell me what this is all about."

Ignoring Seth's indignation, White snapped his briefcase closed. "We'll be at Miss Wyatt's cabin until noon. If you aren't going to charge her, then I'll have someone come by before the close of business today to get those copies."

Seth was still speechless and angry as he watched Peter White, Esquire, escort a silent Savannah from the building. He moved to the window and watched as White put Savannah in the passenger's side of a government-issue vehicle. His head was swimming. Savannah must have used her phone call the previous night to call the Feds. What did she have to do with them and why were they in such a hurry to grab jurisdiction?

One possibility was that she truly was a serial killer and all this federal mumbo jumbo was just to get her into the hands of the FBI. Seth shook his head to rid it of that idea. His instincts told him that *this* woman just didn't fit the profile.

Savannah had an in with the Feds, but so did he.

Seth grabbed up his coat, left word where he was going and headed out into the painfully bright sunlight glaring off the snowdrifts.

He walked across the street to his brother's medical office. About ten minutes after his arrival, Chance came out into the waiting room and frowned. "You look like hell."

"Yeah?" Seth responded. "Well I feel worse. I was up all night."

"Want to sack out on one of my examination tables?"

Seth shook his head as Chance took him back to his cluttered office. He made an attempt to exchange pleasantries with Val, Chance's nurse and Tara, the billing clerk who worked for Chance, but also moonlighted with Junior during tax season. Chance poured two cups of coffee, then sat on the edge of his desk prepared to listen to Seth's dilemma.

"I heard the butcher's bill went up last night," Chance said.

Seth picked up a plastic heart and started to disassemble it. "Butcher's bill?"

"During the Battle of Trafalgar, Admiral Nelson used to ask his aide for the butcher's bill for the day. He thought it was more humane then asking how many soldiers had died."

"Bill Grayson is currently in the morgue at Deer Lake Hospital," Seth said. He then went on to retell the events leading up to, during and after the discovery of Bill's body.

"Sounds like you've got the Wyatt woman dead to rights—no pun intended."

Seth glared at his younger brother. "I've no longer *got* the Wyatt woman. Some federal attorney was waiting for me when I got back this morning. Tossed a bunch of motions at me, then waltzed out of the office with Savannah in tow."

One of Chance's salt-and-pepper brows arched. "Savannah?"

"Yes," Seth hissed, all but daring his sibling to make an issue out of it.

Which was precisely what Chance did. "You've got the hots for a woman who kills her dates? You need some serious counseling, bro."

"I do not have the hots," Seth insisted.

"Pu-lease," Chance said, chuckling. "I can hear it in the way you say her name. Reminds me of when Sam fell for Callie."

"It isn't anything like that," Seth insisted defensively.

That only made Chance laugh harder. "You can fool yourself, but you can't fool your doctor."

"My doctor is a fool," Seth grumbled.

"Very adult, Seth. Name-calling isn't very impressive when it comes from the town's senior law enforcement officer."

Seth took a long sip of the hot coffee. "Okay, so

maybe I've noticed a few things about her that I find appealing."

Chance grinned. "Now we're getting to the good part."

Seth gave his brother a warning look. "I was referring to her personality, not her body."

"Too bad," Chance said, raking his hands through his hair. "Because I've seen her body and it seems flawless to me."

"Chance?"

"She's not a patient," Chance defended with poorly feigned innocence. "Every now and again I run into her on the street. I'm not sure whether it's her pouty lips or those blue-brown eyes that excite—"

"Shut up!" Seth wailed.

Chance was laughing at him, which didn't improve Seth's disposition.

"I was only ragging on you to prove a point," Chance explained.

"That point being that in spite of those dozen or so gray hairs, you're still a childish SOB?"

"No," Chance answered, more subdued. "You're thirty-eight years old. It's about time that a woman knocked you to your knees."

"I am not on my knees," Seth insisted. He closed his eyes long enough to let out a slow sigh. "I don't know what I am."

"Why don't you spend some time with her and find out?" Chance suggested.

"I'd have to get in line. White got a federal judge to give him custody of Savannah if she's charged."

"Are you going to charge her?" Chance asked.

"No. In spite of the evidence, which isn't much more substantial than her having been with all three men before their deaths, all my instincts tell me she isn't the killer."

"Do you trust your instincts?" Chance asked, apparently worried for his sibling. "If you're wrong, this woman could decide to make you victim number four."

After a brief moment of reflection, Seth said, "I'm sure. She's not the killer. But I think she might be the reason for the killings."

"What?"

Seth explained about her hidden past and said, "Since she knew how to get herself a Justice Department attorney here almost instantly, I'm thinking that maybe Savannah is the target, not the perpetrator."

"So, what are you going to do?"

"Go out to the ranch, grab a few hours of sleep, then see if I can find some way to get in touch with Cody."

THE LUCKY 7 was 825,000 acres, fifteen miles from downtown Jasper. Unlike Shane and Sam, the ranch no longer felt like home for him. It hadn't for ten years, ever since his mother and father had taken off.

As he drove closer to the ranch, Seth tried to imagine what they'd be doing now and why they had both chosen to sever all contact with their seven sons. That was the part that continued to haunt Seth even after a decade.

He'd been twenty-eight when it happened and for the life of him, he hadn't seen it coming. Hell, he hadn't had the first inkling that there was trouble in the marriage. He did recall that when he was about ten, his parents had had several loud arguments when they assumed the boys were all sleeping. But that seemed to pass and there had been nothing to prepare him ten years later for the announcement that his mother was leaving with some man she would only name as John. Nor could he or any of his siblings talk his father, Caleb, from heading out after Pricilla and the mysterious John.

Seth smiled, thinking back on the great times he had had with his father. Caleb had been a kind and patient father to every one of his sons, except for Shane. For some reason, Shane could do very little to please the old man. Caleb used to taunt Shane about his bruises, calling him a wimpy little brat. Luckily, in the ten years Shane had been off doing whatever, he had gained self-confidence and self-esteem. Ironically, he was now the most like Caleb. He loved the ranch, loved the physical labor, the long hours.

Seth was so lost in thought that he nearly missed

the arched brick-and-wrought-iron gate to the ranch. About a half mile ahead, he could see the house, with smoke curling out of one of the chimneys.

There were tracks in the snow of the front lawn, and deep ridges from a sled. Obviously, his nephew, Kevin, was learning to steer the old sled that had been handmade by his great-grandfather. A true Landry tradition.

Parking the Bronco in the horseshoe-shaped drive, he climbed the steps and hurried inside. He was about dead on his feet.

"Uncle Seth!" Kevin screamed as he came barreling around the corner and into Seth's legs.

Lifting the boy, he gave him a hug and tousled his white-blond hair. Just as he was putting the boy down, Callie, his sister-in-law, sort of waddled in his direction. She was so small that at six months, she looked like most pregnant women in their final days.

Her smile was bright and genuine. He bent down and gave her a kiss. She took his hand and placed it on her swollen abdomen, moving it for a moment until he felt a strong jolt against his hand.

"Wow," was all Seth could manage to murmur.

"Ow is more like it," Callie complained good-naturedly. "This baby's a kicker. Night and day. I'm so tired I can barely stand up."

"I know the feeling," Seth agreed. "I called Sam's office and they said he was working from home today."

"In the den," Callie said. "Shall I ask Taylor to bring in coffee?"

Seth shook his head. "Not for me. After I talk to Sam, I was hoping to sack out in one of the bedrooms."

Callie placed a concerned hand on his arm. "Are you all right?"

He nodded and faked a pretty decent smile. "Just tired."

"Then get whatever you need from Sam and get to bed. I'll let Taylor know you're here in case your office calls."

"Thanks. Ask Taylor to make sure I'm awake before noon."

Seth found his brother in the darkly paneled office looking at a ream or so of computer printouts. Sam glanced up and greeted his brother with a mixture of happiness and curiosity.

"You look a little worse for wear," Sam commented. "I heard about Bill Grayson. Tough thing. You went to school with him, didn't you?"

Seth nodded. "Doc Hall is trying to track down some relatives. With his mother and father gone, we're not sure what to do with his body after the autopsy."

Taylor Reese, the housekeeper, came in carrying a tray and wearing a smile. She was quite a change from their late housekeeper Mrs. Lange. Taylor was a part-time student and to most men, a ravishing beauty.

Ironically, Seth used to think some less than pure thoughts whenever he saw Taylor. Today all he seemed to notice was that she had brought him some red-colored herbal tea that she promised would help him sleep.

Seth thanked her, but had no intention of drinking something that looked like steaming Kool-Aid.

As usual, wherever Taylor was, Shane wasn't too far behind. In fact, when he joined Seth and Sam in the office, his eyes were pretty much glued to Taylor's behind as she left the room.

Shane made an exaggerated gesture of his heart beating rapidly. "I'll wear her down if it takes me the rest of my life."

Seth and Sam exchanged looks. They had a bet riding on any outcome. Seth's fifty was in Shane's corner. "Good luck."

"Thanks," Shane muttered. "What are you doing here? Shouldn't you be at the jail guarding your incredibly beautiful prisoner, Miss Wyatt?"

Seth rolled his eyes. "I thought Taylor was your project. What would you know about Savannah?"

"Savannah?" Shane and Sam said in unison.

Seth blew out a frustrated breath. "That's her name for God's sake!"

Shane moved to the edge of the mahogany desk and leaned against it, then lifted one of the cups of coffee to his mouth.

"What did you do now?" Seth asked when he

saw a portion of a huge purple bruise on Shane's wrist.

His baby brother shrugged. "Musta hit it when I was in one of the corrals. Forget me. Tell me why you're referring to our resident Black Widow killer by her first name."

"She isn't a killer!" Seth insisted.

Both brothers backed off. "Sorry. It's just that the paper said—"

"Sam, *you* ought to know better than to believe everything you read."

"Point taken," his eldest brother agreed. He knew firsthand how easily the truth could be twisted. He and Callie had learned that lesson the hard way.

Seth told his brothers all about the Fowler, Whitlock and Grayson murders, the trophies, his fruitless search of Savannah's place, everything.

"It's a piece of cake to get out of the rooms at the Mountainview Inn without being seen," Shane said.

"How?" Seth asked.

"The ventilation system. All the bathrooms have oversize vents. You just slip in there and follow it to the end of the building. You can even see the parking lot, so you can jump down when you know the coast is clear. The only problem is, you have to be lanky or little to get through. The vents are pretty tight. But if you're sure Savannah wasn't the killer, that would be my guess as to how the murderer escaped right from under your nose."

"And how do you know this, Shane?"

"Ruthie Nestor's cousin LouAnn."

"LouAnn?" Seth asked.

"When she and her family would come to visit the Nestors in the summer, I would go and visit LouAnn at the inn," Shane explained with a guilt-less grin.

Seth picked up the phone and called J.D. and ordered him to check the vents from Grayson's room through the whole building if he had to.

"Thanks," he told Shane.

Shane lifted his coffee mug in mock salute. "To LouAnn."

"So," Sam began cautiously. "What's the deal with you and the Wyatt woman?"

"There is no deal," Seth insisted. Though just hearing her name was enough to remind him of the feel of her warm skin as his knuckles brushed her nape when he'd helped her on with her coat. His body started to react, so he quickly dismissed the thoughts. "I need to get in touch with Cody."

"Why?" Shane asked.

"Because right now Savannah is in the custody of the Feds. Cody is a Fed and I want some answers."

"What about asking Savannah?" Sam suggested.

"Pointless," Seth insisted. "Whatever secrets she has, she's keeping them pretty close."

Reaching into the desk, Sam retrieved his phone

book and handed it to Seth. Cody's name appeared once, but there were more than a dozen phone numbers scratched out on the page. Seth dialed the only one left unmarked.

"U.S. Marshal's Office, how may I direct your call?"

"I'd like to speak to Marshal Cody Landry. This is his brother, Seth Landry."

"Hold, please."

Seth broke down and tasted some of the cranberry-colored tea while he waited.

The female voice came back on the line, "I'm sorry but he's out on assignment right now."

"If he calls in for messages, would you please tell him to call me at work or at the ranch."

"Does he have those numbers, sir?"

"Yes."

"Thank you."

The line went dead right along with Seth's brain. "I need a couple of hours of sleep," Seth said. "Somebody get me if either J.D. or Cody calls, okay?"

They agreed and Seth sluggishly carried himself up to his old room. On the way he passed Chance's old room. All the academic awards and dated posters were gone, replaced with stenciled bunnies and a crib awaiting the arrival of the next Landry. If he didn't get a grip, Sam might single-handedly re-populate the ten-bedroom home.

Seth pulled off his boots and fell across the down mattress without bothering to turn down the covers. He was fast asleep a second after his head hit the pillow.

For more than two hours, his dreams were filled with visions of Savannah. He even imagined she was calling to him.

"…Seth?" The female voice seemed almost real. "Seth!"

Realizing it was real, he sat bolt upright in the bed. "What?"

Taylor nervously drew her lip between her teeth. "Sorry to wake you but—"

"The phone?"

She nodded, but when he started to get up she said, "Don't hurry, Cody already hung up."

*"What?"*

## Chapter Six

Even though it had been an hour since Cody Landry had called the ranch, Savannah still wasn't prepared for Seth's furious expression when he stormed through the door.

Peter White drew back, but Cody stood his ground, until Seth rammed him hard against the kitchen wall.

"Is this necessary?" Savannah asked, hoping to avoid violence between the siblings.

"Why did you keep me out of the loop?" Seth demanded. He held Cody by the lapels of his dark suit coat. "If you had information about the murders, why didn't you let me know?"

Cody remained impassively silent.

Seth gave him a gentle shake. "Why, dammit?"

For Savannah, it all went a little too quickly. Somehow, Seth had gone from being the aggressor, trapping Cody against the wall, to having his arm twisted high behind his back by Cody.

"Calm down," was all Cody said. It was spoken softly, but it was definitely a command.

Seth struggled briefly, then surrendered, though Savannah saw a dangerous glint in his ebony eyes.

"I'm calm," Seth relented, then was let free.

Savannah was standing over by the green-and-white chair, loading things into an open moving carton.

"What are you doing?" he asked her.

"Packing."

She watched as Seth looked at Peter White, then Cody, then fixed those dark eyes on her. "Care to tell me what's going on?"

She saw a flicker of emotion cross Cody's otherwise granite face. Peter just seemed to be his usual superior self. Savannah had never really liked Peter, even though she had him to thank for still being alive. He was one of those guys who was a little too smooth, a little too cocky for her tastes.

Cody wasn't much of an improvement. Every conversation she had with him made her feel as if she had stepped into a rerun of Tom Hanks and Dan Aykroyd in *Dragnet. Yes, ma'am. No ma'am. I'm afraid we can't disclose that location, ma'am.*

It seemed pitifully ironic that of the three men in

the room, Seth was her preference. Probably because she had sort of gotten to know him. They had had one conversation. Not counting the times when he was busy accusing her of murder.

"Miss Wyatt is in federal custody," Peter announced as casually as he might have said "This cabin is made of logs."

"For what?" Seth asked, purposefully directing his question to Cody.

"I'm afraid the marshal—" Peter began.

"Why don't you go check the oil in your car?" Cody suggested. His tone alone sent Peter out into the cold. "That guy is a real dipstick," he said as soon as the Justice Department attorney was out of earshot.

It was the first time Savannah had heard Cody say anything spontaneous and unofficial. It was a side of him she hadn't seen to this point in their years of acquaintance.

"So what's going on?" Seth urged.

"The Rossi crime family," Cody said.

Seth held up his hands, apparently needing more information.

"Miss Wyatt is our only witness to how the Rossi family was importing and distributing cocaine and heroine."

She quaked just hearing the name of the infamous New York crime syndicate.

Seth looked at her, his expression one of total disbelief.

She stopped stuffing hatboxes into the container and said, "Thanks to the ongoing investigation from hell, continuances, motions, search warrants, wiretaps, attorneys, and the death of the only other witness, I've been in hiding for almost six years. And Peter says we still aren't anywhere near ready for trial," she told him bitterly.

Seth turned to his brother. "Why in the hell didn't you tell me you were stashing one of your witnesses in my jurisdiction?"

"We don't advertise," Cody retorted. "I just hadn't figured on them making three attempts on her life in three weeks."

"They weren't attempts on my life," Savannah grumbled.

"She's right," Seth agreed.

Savannah was surprised and relieved to finally have someone on her side. Or at least willing to look at the overall picture. Thank heavens Seth shared her line of thought. If the Rossis wanted her dead, they'd have killed her, not her dates.

"What do you call Fowler, Whitlock and Grayson?" Peter countered when he returned, blowing hot breath into his obviously freezing hands.

Seth went over to the sofa and sat down to gather his thoughts. "If Savannah was the target in the Grayson shooting, she'd have been dead on the floor when I broke down the door."

"You don't know that," Peter argued. "Perhaps the killer was held up taking Grayson out and didn't have the chance to get to Miss Wyatt when you arrived. Or maybe this is a more elaborate plan. The Rossis frame Savannah for murder and her usefulness to me as a witness is null."

"Gee, thanks," Savannah snapped.

Cody and Seth exchanged a silent communication that wasn't hard to read. Obviously Cody had respect for his brother's opinions and found Peter's murder setup scheme too far-out to be realistic.

"Okay," Seth began again, speaking more slowly to Peter, as if he was an errant child. "Richard Fowler, the first victim and Harvey Whitlock the second one, remember them?"

"Yes?" Peter answered hotly.

"They were found floating in Brock Creek. Which, in case you don't have a map, doesn't run within ten miles of this cabin. The currents are fairly strong north of the inn."

"Meaning?" Peter challenged.

"Meaning they were killed by the inn. Savannah always drove her own car to the inn. Meaning if someone wanted to kill her, they could have killed her and not bothered with the men she had dinner with. But that didn't happen, now did it?"

Savannah cringed at the memories.

"Then there's the matter of the trophies," Seth continued, virtually chastising her government attorney. "Our killer took a medal from Fowler, gems from Grayson and something from Whitlock."

"What *something?*" Cody asked.

She heard Seth sigh. "We haven't had much luck tracing Whitlock. Haven't even been able to locate next of kin to figure out what personal item might be missing. But I guarantee something of Whitlock's is in the possession of the killer."

"I can work on that," Cody said.

Seth nodded. "I'll give you everything I've got. Whitlock's personal effects and the inventory from his house."

"Keep packing, Miss Wyatt," Peter insisted, apparently ignoring the brothers Landry.

"You're making her leave when you don't even have all the facts?" Seth asked.

"Of course. I'm not going to let six years of investigative work go down the drain."

"Not to mention keeping me alive," Savannah reminded him curtly. "That was the purpose for disrupting my entire life, right?"

Seth rose and went to her. When he spoke, she could feel his warm breath on her face. "Do you want to leave?"

He took her hand, making it impossible for her to speak, so she just shook her head.

"She has no choice," Peter said. "She's a material witness."

"She's an American citizen," Seth retorted.

"She'll testify when the time comes, but until then, she stays here. With me."

Savannah wasn't sure which of them was more shocked. She had never expected Seth to come to her aid like that and judging by the look on his face, it was a purely spontaneous decision on his part.

Savannah was sent to her bedroom so the three men could talk privately in the kitchen. Her pulse was racing so fast she could hear it drumming in her ears.

*Stay in one place for a while?* she thought excitedly. With Seth as my guardian? That thought was more than exciting. It caused a little thrill in the pit of her stomach. She paced the room like a caged animal waiting to be set free.

"Stop this!" she hissed in a harsh whisper. "What if I stay with Seth and they *do* know where I am? I could get Seth killed." That thought made her heart skip a beat. "But his argument to Peter made so much sense. If someone wanted to kill me instead of my dates, they had every opportunity."

With Richard Fowler, they could have just waited here at the cabin and killed her when she arrived home. With Harvey, she was a moving target from the time she left him on the bridge until she made it to her car. Savannah's mind swirled. She all but raced from the room.

The three men fell silent the instant she arrived, mildly breathless. "Seth is right."

"We can't chance it," Peter said. "You could be compromised."

She stopped long enough to glare at the preppy annoyance. "*If* someone wanted to kill me, they've had a hundred opportunities since I moved here. I take classes two nights a week and I work every weekday at a shop in town."

"You were told to blend into the community," Peter admonished. "Not make yourself a presence."

"A job and taking classes has made me blend. Look around you, Peter. If I stayed here and lived off my savings, don't you think the townspeople would be suspicious?"

"You haven't broken the contact rule, have you?"

Savannah lowered her eyes. "I haven't called my family from here."

"Nice operation you run," she heard Seth remark to Cody. "I guess Christmas and birthdays are out, too."

"Don't push me," she heard Cody warn. "I'm going to authorize this."

"What!" Peter almost imploded. "You're going to leave the safety of my only witness in the hands of some hick-town sheriff?"

"No," Cody said calmly. "I'm leaving her in the capable hands of my big brother. You got a problem with that?"

Some of Peter's indignation seemed to drain. "She needs to be in a safe house where we can check on her—"

"You mean smother her," Cody commented. "Look, we did that to her for a year. I think it's best to leave her here in Jasper, at least while we check into the murders. They may not even be connected to the Rossi investigation."

"I think you're deluding yourself, Marshal," Peter groused. "So what do you suggest we do?" Peter demanded of Seth. "Deputize her so she can go to work with you? She needs to be watched constantly."

"Don't worry, Mr. White," Seth drawled. "I'm sure my deputies can handle my little hick town while I devote myself to keeping your witness alive."

"You'd better," Peter warned. "If I lose her, I lose my whole case."

"We can't have that," Seth said. Turning to Cody he said, "Stop by my office for the evidence. I'll call Mable now and make sure she has it ready."

The two men shook hands, then gave one armed hugs and slaps on the back before parting ways. Peter simply stuffed his ungloved hands in his pockets and stomped out into the snow.

This was it. She was alone with Seth. This was how it was going to be. Oddly, as she looked into his eyes, she wondered just how long it would be before she fell in love with him. Painfully, she knew that even if that happened, there was nothing she could do about it. As soon as she did her civic duty, she was going back home to her family. One look at

Seth told her that his roots were firmly planted in the rugged beauty of Jasper. She would never put him in the position of asking him to leave his hometown. Not when she knew all too well the pain of abandoning everything and everyone familiar.

Seth grabbed the phone and called his office as promised. J.D. still hadn't returned from his crawl through the inn's ventilation system, but Mable would make sure all the nonemergency calls were handled by J.D. or Greg, the other deputy. Then, surprising her, Seth told her to call in the state police on anything big, just to keep him apprized by radio or phone. It sounded as if Mable was trying to get more than that out of him, but Seth was tight-lipped.

He hung up the phone and looked over at Savannah, who was busy taking everything out of the carton and putting everything back in place. "Tell me about the no-contact rule," Seth said.

She met his eyes. "I'm not allowed to contact my family in case the Rossi family has tapped the lines."

He held her gaze. "So you were technically honest when you told White you hadn't called from here."

Savannah was wringing her hands, but he thought she had one hell of a poker face. "Of course I was telling the truth."

"About this cabin," Seth sighed, then raked his hair back. "You didn't tell him about the pay phone outside the post office."

She seemed genuinely shocked.

"I'm not a stupid man, Savannah," he warned. "Remember that in the future."

"How did you know?" she asked without apology.

"I watched you stuff coins in the phone. Then I got the LUDs from the phone company."

"LUDs?"

"Local usage details. You called a business listing in Norwalk, Connecticut."

Savannah hung her head. "My mother's office." Savannah lifted her face to his. "But I never spoke to her. I just listened to her voice and hung up."

"Let me call Cody and square this with him. I'm sure they can check to see if there's any tap on your mother's office phone."

Savannah ran over and grasped his powerful biceps through his shirt. Frantically, she asked, "I didn't put my mother in danger, did I?"

Seth patted her hand, relishing in the feel of her touch, even if it was brief and in a moment of panic. Lord but she smelled good. Standing next to her, Seth could feel the heat from her small frame. It would have taken very little effort to move his hand to her waist, turn her a whisper to the left and place a kiss on her slightly parted lips.

*Great, now I'm thinking with my slightly parted brain!* Seth made sure Cody knew about Savannah's transgression. Then he suggested they go for a drive.

"Where?" she asked warily.

"I need to go to my place and pack a bag."

"You don't have to sleep here," she said.

"Yes, I do," he countered. "I'll pack a bag, and make us something to eat, then we'll come back for the night."

"Handsome and he cooks," Savannah teased. "If you also do all the cleaning and the laundry, you're the man my mother told me to marry."

Seth cleared his throat nervously. "I don't think I'm marriage material."

Savannah gave him a gentle nudge as they walked out the door. "I was making a joke, Seth, not a proposal."

She climbed up into the Bronco. When Seth got behind the wheel, she said, "You know, the last time I was in this truck, you took me to jail and ordered my complete humiliation."

Seth felt the words jab him like a knife. "I was just doing my job."

"I know," she agreed easily.

More easily than he would have if their positions had been reversed.

"If you didn't think I was guilty, why put me through that?" she asked softly.

"I'm sorry, Savannah. But I can't write a report saying I failed to follow procedure because I *personally* don't think the suspect is guilty."

"Okay," she relented quickly.

When he drove past the Mountainview Inn, he

noticed Savannah suffer a nervous jolt. Not knowing what to do, he simply placed his hand on her denim-clad knee. Almost instantly, Savannah laced her fingers through his. Seth wasn't sure how to handle this. Part of him knew that he should be hands-off, yet that other part of him begged for this to be the beginning of something. *But what?* Could he stand being with a woman who could be killed or could disappear as abruptly as his mother? Was it worth it? And what guarantee did he have that once she testified, she wouldn't go running back to Connecticut? Another possible form of abandonment. Could he stand it? He glanced over at Savannah's exquisite face and the answer came to him in a flash. *Yes.*

Seth showed her inside his home. It was a western-style brick two-story. For some reason, it mattered to him what she thought of it. He didn't have to wait long.

"Who knew you could decorate in roadkill and hide?" she asked with false sweetness.

"I used to hunt back in the days when it was politically correct," Seth explained a little defensively.

Savannah pointed to the mounted animals and said, "In honor of giving up that barbaric sport, have you considered taking down the glass-eyed heads that follow you everywhere?"

"I don't recall me making fun of your fake birdcage."

She seemed stunned that he had noticed the

detail. "The important word there is *fake*. I have all fake furs, nothing had to die for me to decorate."

"Well, maybe I'll get around to it. Come on upstairs. The second floor is a dead-thing-free zone."

"Okay."

Hearing her soft chuckle was a salve for his unusually frazzled nerves. He hadn't felt this self-conscious since the tenth grade when he'd lured Melanie Yount beneath the bleachers at a high school football game. What was it about this woman that had him forever off-kilter?

He had the oddest conflicting emotions when Savannah entered his bedroom. She was the first woman ever to be in the room *not* for the specific purpose of seduction. It was strange. It got worse when she made herself right at home by climbing up on his high iron-and-post bed and tested the mattress. Her wriggling body in the center of his bed raised his blood pressure, among other things. Her green sweater had ridden up so that he could see the outline of her rib cage as well as a glint when her belly button ring caught the light.

"This is comfortable," she sighed, testing his mattress.

*Not for me.* Seth began throwing clothing into a bag. He was so flustered that he had to stop, dump everything out and start again.

"Need help?" Savannah called from his bed.

"No."

She rolled over, slid to the end of the bed and rested her chin on her hands, watching him intently. Though he was a big man, there was nothing at all bulky or awkward about him. In fact, watching muscle strain against the fabric of his tan uniform reminded Savannah of watching a prized thorough-bred going through its paces.

He was graceful, yet very powerfully built. One of his thighs was probably an equal circumference to her waist. But there seemed to be a gentleness about him that belied the raw strength. Or perhaps there was just something totally nonthreatening about watching a man fold his boxer shorts, she thought with private humor.

Savannah was a little surprised when he went to his closet and collected some civilian clothes to add to the duffel-shaped bag. Well, soon enough she'd know whether it was the uniform or the man that so attracted her.

Seth zipped the bag and hoisted it onto his shoulder as if it were weightless. Turning to her, he asked, "Hungry?"

*Not necessarily for food,* she thought. Prudence made her respond with a polite and prim, "Yes."

He led her down into a kitchen she could only describe as masculine and rustic. Judging from the thin layer of dust on the sideboard, he didn't enter-tain much. Which could mean he didn't date much. *Which could mean I'm obsessing about this man!*

Seth opened the freezer, then the refrigerator compartment. He emerged holding a bag of preprepared salad and a bottle of white wine. "How does chicken Caesar salad sound?"

"Fine," she answered.

Savannah pulled out one of the chairs to sit at the long, battered pine table and accepted the corkscrew and bottle from Seth. He then went back to the freezer and pulled yet another bag of precooked food out.

While he prepared to heat the grilled chicken strips on the stove, Savannah went in search of wineglasses. She started at the sideboard and went still when she saw the collection of photographs up close.

"I don't think I fully understood seven children until this instant." She picked up an eleven-by-fourteen group shot and guessed it was close to twenty years old. Sam, Chance and Seth were easily recognizable, even though twenty years ago Dr. Landry hadn't had his prematuring gray temples or eyebrows.

"Just think herd," Seth joked. "I'll never know how my mother stood all of us."

She reached out and touched the only female face in the picture. "What is her name?"

"Pricilla," Seth said.

Hearing the slight catch in his voice broke her heart. Savannah could relate. It was the reason she kept all reminders of her family carefully stored out of sight. She couldn't bear seeing their images, knowing she couldn't contact them.

The woman was incredibly beautiful and you'd never know she'd given birth to seven boys. She was tall, elegant, with dark coloring and the same half smile she had passed on to her offspring.

She remembered Seth telling her his father's name was Caleb. He, too, was an attractive man. He had his hands on the shoulders of two of his sons. "Who are these?" she asked, holding up the picture and pointing to them.

"Chandler and Clayton," Seth answered.

Savannah wanted to kick herself. She'd asked two simple questions and both had caused Seth varying degrees of pain. Clayton was in prison, and she knew from his earlier blowup that it wasn't something Seth liked to think or talk about.

The youngest child was Shane. He stood in front of his mother, smiling even though he had a big bruise on the side of his face. Savannah wondered which one of his older brothers was responsible for that.

Though he had changed a great deal in twenty years, by process of elimination, she knew the one standing next to Chance had to be Cody. She smiled. He was stiff and rigid, even as a child.

"Dinner is served," Seth called.

She turned to see that he had set the table, poured

the wine, and had two plates full and waiting for consumption.

"Sorry, I should have helped."

"You did. You opened the wine."

Savannah rolled her eyes. "Oh, major contribution," she responded with good-natured sarcasm. She took her seat and Seth grabbed the end chair. The one closest to her. It was a huge table, but having him so near suddenly made the table feel about the same size as a matchbox.

She tasted the salad and had to admit, it was a lot better than anything she could have thrown together in less than ten minutes. She told Seth as much. "I'm basically dependent upon takeout and Olive for sustenance," she confessed. "She's forever bringing over baked goods. Or sending Junior out with whatever leftovers they have."

"Olive's a nice lady," Seth said. "Junior is a little weird, but then that's to be expected, given his past."

Savannah peered over at him. "His past?" she asked before taking another bite of food.

Seth nodded. "He was always a bit of a dork growing up. But his father seemed to keep Olive's… *smothering* tendencies at bay. Until he died in a hunting accident when Junior was thirteen."

"How terrible!" Savannah said. "That's a very difficult age for a boy to lose his father."

"Especially since he saw the accident," he said, then shrugged off the memory.

His eyes were fixed on her face. Suddenly, the temperature in the room seemed to go up a few degrees Fahrenheit. His hand snaked out and she felt the startling thrill of the pad of his thumb against her lower lip.

She was so shocked by the unexpected contact, all she could do was suck in a hurried gasp of air.

"You have dressing here," he said. His voice was deep, sensual and as mesmerizing as his dark eyes.

His thumb ran the full length of her lip as his palm cradled her jaw. He did it once, twice, increasing the pressure each time. By the third pass, Savannah was perspiring. His simple action had been more seductive, more intimate than a kiss. She felt abandoned when he pulled his hand back. More than that, she felt an overwhelming urge to reach out and drag him to her. *That* would be even better.

"Better?" Seth asked.

# *Chapter Seven*

Her eyes were pools of unspent blue-brown passion. Seth should have known better than to touch her that way. His initial motivation had been pure, but the instant his thumb felt the full softness of her rosy lip, he just couldn't help himself. Nor could he help his body's quick response.

Adjusting his napkin in his lap, he knew a change of topic was the only thing that would distract him from the unimaginable desire he felt for Savannah. Unfortunately for him, it wasn't just the physical attraction that worried him.

It was knowing, deep down, that he was beginning to feel something that he'd never before felt. And that was scary as hell.

Abandoning his plate, he grabbed his wine and took a fortifying sip. "So, since you know all about my family, why don't you tell me about yours?"

He had hoped his tactic would distract her. Instead, his question left an unmistakable glint of sorrow in her exquisite eyes. Despite whatever private emotion she might be feeling, Savannah offered him a smile that made him glad he was sitting down. *Lord but she was ravishing when she smiled.* It had to have something to do with the way her unusual coloring came together to form exotic perfection. Her skin was pale, but had a faint olive tinge, suggesting one of her ancestors was Latin or maybe Italian. Her shoulder-length hair was several shades lighter than his own, maybe medium brown, and parted on the left side.

There were times he was sure she wasn't aware that her hair fell forward, nearly covering her right eye. It gave her a sexy look—sort of like a dark-haired version of the popular forties actress Veronica Lake. In the correct light, her hair had some auburn highlights, the type he knew many women paid dearly for. Hers were definitely natural, just like her innate beauty.

"Hello?" he heard Savannah's voice question.

"Sorry," Seth mumbled, not realizing that he had been ignoring her while cataloging her many assets. "Please tell me about your family."

"Savannah is my real first name," she explained.

"My parents named me after the city where they met."

Seth smiled. "Then I'm sure you can guess why my one brother's name is Chance—my folks took one."

She laughed. The mere sound of her laughter filling his home seemed somehow comforting, right.

"I have three younger brothers. All of them are in college now."

"Then I don't need to bother checking out the picture I took from your cabin of you standing with your family at one of the boy's high school graduation."

Savannah's expression changed instantly. Her eyes blazed. "You took one of my photographs?"

He reached for her hand, but she snatched it out of reach. "At the time, you were the prime suspect in three murders. I'll get it back to you tomorrow. Chill out."

She did, but slowly. "The boys are, in descending order, Matthew, Mark and Luke."

"Your family is religious?" Seth guessed.

Savannah shrugged. "They go to church. But the names came about because after me, my parents were told they couldn't have any more children. So, six years later, when the boys all came within twenty months, they figured the boys were gifts from God, hence their names."

Seth gave a half laugh. "My parents started out

giving us names beginning with *S,* because Pop always called mom Silla in stead of Pricilla. But when we kept coming and coming and coming, they switched to *C*s, for my father, Caleb. Except for Shane. I suppose by the time he came along they had run out of names beginning with the letter *C.*" Seth took another sip of wine and felt himself relaxing for the first time since they had fished Fowler's body out of Brock Creek. "You said you called your mother's office. Is she a secretary?"

Now Savannah gave a chuckle. "Not *my* mother. Not that there's anything wrong with secretarial work, but Patricia Hale-Smythe is just one of those holdovers from the feminist movement. She believed and wanted it all. She owns her own interior decorating business. Makes almost as much a year as my father."

"Who is…?"

"Conway Smythe, M.D., one of the busiest OB-GYNs in Norwalk, Connecticut."

Seth whistled. "So we have something in common."

Her brows wrinkled. "What?"

"We both come from financially…*comfortable* backgrounds."

Savannah huffed. "I'd hardly relate the Smythe family with the vast holdings of the Landrys. By the way, do you know Junior's only wish in life is to handle your family's finances?"

"That wouldn't sit too well with Sam," Seth

remarked. "I don't see my financial-analyst brother turning over the family business to a CPA."

"Junior's good with money," Savannah defended mildly.

"How do you know?"

"When they put me into the Witness Protection Program, my father liquidated a small trust fund he'd set up for me. So Savannah Wyatt has to pay quarterly taxes on Savannah Smythe's money. Junior helps me."

"I thought the Feds paid all your relocation expenses. Does Junior know you're actually Savannah Smythe?"

"Absolutely not. The Feds made Savannah Smythe's money turn into Savannah Wyatt's money. Junior doesn't have the first clue. Having my own money meant I could finish college when they had me in Maryland. And continue now that I'm in Montana. I just had a lot of work to make up since I had to totally change my career plans."

Seth recalled the sketches he had seen in her cabin. "You were an art major?"

"Fashion design," she corrected. "I was going to be the Vera Wang of the new millennium. Which is how I got into this mess."

Seth refilled their glasses. "Sorry, but I didn't know that mobsters were into fashion design. Well, except for that Gotti guy, but he'll be wearing prison issue for the rest of his days."

Savannah's smile reached her eyes and melted his insides. Seth downed nearly half of the contents of his glass and hoped she didn't notice the slight tremble in his hand. This woman had him so off balance he'd probably fall out of his chair at any moment. If it registered, he could see no outward signs. Which soured his mood slightly. Was it because she knew she had this sort of effect on men? Any man? *Him?*

"I was attending college in Manhattan," Savannah began to explain. "Being the impatient type—" she paused to offer a guilty smile "—I didn't want to wait the three months for graduation to start looking for a job. So, I applied to a small design house, hoping to get some experience before I approached Calvin Klein or one of the other fashion icons."

"Good plan."

Savannah sighed. "Not really. This house put me to work in cutting. Which is a logical entry-level job. Tough on the hands, though. And still being the impatient sort, I decided to stay late with my friend Brenda, who was also about to graduate."

"Was Brenda the other witness?"

Savannah gave a slow, solemn nod. "We had delusions of grandeur. We were going to impress our boss by designing a dress using some of the beads we found rummaging around the warehouse. They were just piled in boxes as high as the warehouse ceiling, so we figured borrowing a few wouldn't be a problem."

"Only the boxes were full of dope?" Seth asked.

"No, they were much too smart for that. The beads were used on a line of ethnic blouses made in a different part of the warehouse and shipped mainly to discount stores—or so we thought."

"But the beads weren't beads?"

"Right," Savannah said on a quick breath. "Brenda and I had this brilliant idea to cut them in half to decorate the neckline and a matching belt for our dress. Only, when we cut them, some disintegrated into white powder and others were a sticky black goo inside."

"Cocaine and heroine," Seth correctly guessed.

Savannah nodded. "Like fools, instead of quitting, we went to the authorities."

Seth reached for her hand again, this time she didn't pull back. "You did the right thing."

Savannah closed her free hand over his, sandwiching his big hand between her much smaller ones. "My intellect knows that, but the price we paid was too high. Brenda was gunned down in a drive-by when the Feds were moving her to a safe house. I spent a year cooped up in a Manhattan apartment. I couldn't leave the apartment or even go near the windows. Worst of all, I couldn't contact my family. The best I could do was send notes through the federal marshals I had with me at all times. But it wasn't like the post office. I later learned that they held my letters, repackaged them and oftentimes it would take more than six months for my parents to get word from me."

"Was Cody with you all that time?" Seth asked.

"Not until they moved me west," Savannah answered. "When I was in Maryland, I had two female agents who got to go to college with me."

"Why?"

"Well, the Feds tell me I can't ever go back into design because the Rossi family will be watching for me. They set me up in Maryland as a waitress in a trendy bar in Annapolis. That was supposed to be my new life. Savannah Burton, waitress."

"Burton?"

She smiled without humor. "What can I say, the Feds like handing out new identities. They about had a fit when I refused to change my first name."

Seth imagined his hard-line brother in such a situation and instantly understood her point. "The Feds are a rather by-the-rules group, aren't they?"

She nodded. "Yep, but I changed the rules."

"How?"

"Working as a waitress or in Olive's shop is good, honest work. Work I don't mind doing until I can earn my Ph.D. in forensic psychology. It's called self-direction. Since I'm going to have to be someone else, *I'm* going to define that someone, *not* the federal government."

He was impressed. "Is that how you know Taylor?"

"Taylor Reese?" Savannah asked.

"Yes."

Savannah eyed him cautiously. "So, when you thought I was a killer you had me followed? Yes, I know Taylor. We have the same classes and the same advisor, Molly Jameson."

"I didn't have you followed," Seth told her. "Taylor is the housekeeper out at the ranch, remember?"

Savannah appeared to be a touch embarrassed. "Sorry, I forgot. I guess I just don't think of you as a rancher."

"Good," Seth sighed. "Don't get me wrong, I love the land and the heritage that goes with it. I'm just not cut out for the day to day of managing the place, which is why I was thrilled when Shane came back."

He checked his watch, recorked the half-full bottle of wine and put it into the fridge. "We'd better head back to your cabin."

When he turned around, he brushed against her body as she attempted to pass him, her arms loaded with dishes. For Seth it was like being hit with a stun gun. His whole body tingled.

"See," Savannah said, her eyes lowered, "those waitressing days paid off. I didn't drop your plates."

*Plates?* He would have given anything if she'd

pitched them to the floor and leapt into his arms.
*I have got to get a grip!*

SAVANNAH COULD HEAR the telephone ringing as
she put the key in the door, opened it, then made a
dash for the phone. "Hello?"

"Miss Wyatt, this is J.D. Is the sheriff there?"

"Right here," Savannah said. She offered the
phone to Seth, simply saying, "J.D."

Secretly, she was glad for the few moments to
collect herself. As her brother Matthew liked to say,
she was thinking impure thoughts. Glancing over
her shoulder at Seth, she figured it was no wonder.
The man gave new definition to the term *gorgeous*.
He had a kind of subtle sensuality that had her
hormones racing at Indy 500 speeds. If they were
going to occupy the same space for the foreseeable
future, she was going to have to learn to control
herself.

Easier said than done, she thought as she watched
him rake his hand through his thick black hair. In
spite of his efforts, several ebony strands fell
forward to mingle with his inky lashes. Even when
his jaw went taut suddenly, his expression becoming
rather fierce, Savannah still found him dangerously
attractive. Seth was an odd combination of gentleness and blatant sexuality. He didn't even have to
touch her in order for her to feel the awakening of
her desires.

It had been forever since she'd been in a man's arms, so she tried to tell herself that was the sole reason she found Seth so appealing. It had nothing to do with the fact that the more she got to know him—know the little chinks in his armor—the more attracted she was to him.

Unlike his brother Cody, Seth wasn't a blob of macho values. He was strong, yes. She'd even seen him get physical with Cody, but she couldn't find one reason to be afraid of the big man.

Except for the fact that in all probability, she'd be leaving him behind at the whim of the government. Her heart actually hurt at the thought. Montana was temporary; thus, anything she started with Seth would be temporary.

She couldn't risk falling in love with someone when she might be whisked out of his life at any second. She'd disappeared once, to keep her family safe, and it still caused her pain. Savannah didn't think she could do it again in this lifetime and survive.

It seemed natural to have him in her home. It was as if he belonged there, she thought as he hung up the phone. Belonged with her. Good Lord, maybe it was already too late. *Was it possible to fall in love with someone in a matter of days?*

"Don't look so frantic," Seth said, his tone soothing.

"I'm not," Savannah told him, pushing the frightening thoughts from her head. If only she could talk to her mother. Get some advice on what she was feeling. She forced a smile. "How is J.D.?"

"Dusty," Seth answered with a wicked but very, very sexy half smile. "Apparently the Mountainview Inn doesn't routinely clean out the ventilation system."

Savannah tried not to think about sex or sexy. "Is that good or bad?" she asked with feigned brightness.

"Good," Seth said. "The only shafts they found dust free were those around Grayson's room. The bad news is the vents are made of a material we can't dust for prints because the surface is too rough."

"Oh."

"But we did get the results of the prints back from Grayson's room. Nothing there. Just Grayson's and a partial of Junior's on the doorknob."

"Junior's?" Savannah asked.

Seth smiled. "I didn't want to tell you this, but Junior and Bill had a conversation in his room before you arrived. Junior told me himself that he'd made it clear to Grayson that you were going to be Grayson's dinner partner, period."

Savannah felt her cheeks warm to a blush. "I suppose that's very sweet, even though it wasn't necessary."

Seth's expression went still. "You wouldn't have…have… Bill was a nice-looking guy and all, and—"

"Stop stumbling over yourself, Seth," Savannah teased. "No, I would not have gone to bed with Bill Grayson. I don't do one-night stands, even as a favor to Olive."

She liked the fact that he looked relieved. Did that mean that he had feelings for her, or just that he had feelings about one-night stands? The man was confusing the hell out of her!

"There is some interesting news, as well."

"What?"

"A few hours after we finished up at the crime scene, one of the bellmen caught Cal Nestor and a friend in the ventilation system, trying to get a peek into the room."

Savannah shivered. "Remind me never to stay there. Apparently anyone can climb through the inn at will."

Seth shook his head. "Cal Nestor is trouble. I'm sure once he heard there was a murder, he couldn't resist crawling through the vents to take a look."

"Who is Cal Nestor?"

"Jasper's resident juvenile delinquent. And if it wasn't so late, I'd go over there right now and give him a little attitude adjustment."

"Nestor?" Savannah repeated. "Any relation to the waitress at the Cowboy Café?"

"She's his mother. Ruthie tries, but Cal's the kind of kid that needs an iron fist and Ruthie doesn't have one. The kicker is, the kid has a near-genius IQ."

"So why is he always in trouble?"

Seth shrugged. "Ask my brother Shane. He was the same way. Smart as sin and a magnet for trouble. Hopefully Cal will straighten himself up like Shane did." He stifled a yawn.

Savannah realized it was after midnight and that Seth hadn't slept the night before. "Give me a minute to change the sheets on the bed for you."

"I'm taking the couch."

Savannah glared at him, her hands on her hips. "That's idiotic, Seth. You're over six feet tall. I'm barely five-three. I'll take the sofa, you'll take the bed. This isn't open for discussion."

He opened his mouth as if to argue but she warned him off with a pointed stare. Savannah spent about fifteen minutes changing sheets and making herself a bed on the sofa. Her final act was to put several logs on the fireplace and build a fire.

Seth still lingered in the living room. If ever Savannah had had an awkward moment, this was it. Her libido wanted to give him a kiss good-night, but her intelligence made sure that she kept her distance and simply made a shooing motion toward the bed-room. Seth checked all the locks, then disappeared inside her bedroom.

Savannah changed into her nightgown, laying her jeans and sweater over the chair, then slipped into the makeshift bed. She watched the dancing flames for a long, long time before she was able to forget that Seth was in the house.

She fell into a fitful sleep, battling dreams of Rossi, the photograph of Brenda after the shooting, and Bill Grayson's cold dead eyes.

SETH OPENED HIS EYES in the predawn, momentarily disoriented. Probably because he wasn't used to sleeping in a cramped double bed with a frilly eyelet coverlet and floral arrangements everywhere.

Or maybe he was just distracted because the pillow he was holding carried Savannah's scent. Loneliness crept up on him. It was a new experience. He'd been sleeping alone for thirty-eight years, save for the occasional transgression. Normally, he enjoyed the solace and quiet of being alone. But not on this particular dawn. As he watched the sun paint the distant peaks purple, then pink, then finally an orange-yellow, he silently acknowledged why he was feeling lonely for the first time in his life.

Because he'd gone to bed feeling that way. He had listened to Savannah move about in the living room for a long time. He didn't dare hope that her restlessness came from the same place as his own. He'd never know since he couldn't very well walk out into the living room and say, "Since I'm really attracted to you and we're going to be roommates, why don't we just sleep together?" Seth punched the pillow in frustration before rising.

After brushing his teeth, he got his jeans out of his duffel, pulled them on, then quietly walked across the light-olive painted wooden floor. It was incredibly chilly, making him sorry he hadn't put on his boots, but he didn't want to wake Savannah.

Carefully, he turned the knob until he heard the faint click of the latch. Silently he cursed when the hinges squeaked as he opened the bedroom door.

Cold air greeted him when he looked out into the living room. His next curse was no longer silent.

Savannah wasn't on the sofa and the front door stood wide open.

## Chapter Eight

Seth quickly raced back into the bedroom to get his gun. At the same moment, he heard footsteps entering the house. With his gun drawn, he returned to the living room.

Savannah was so startled by either him or the gun or both, that she dropped the bundle of firewood she'd been holding. The logs hit the rug with a muffled thud.

He was standing just inches away from her. It was impossible for him not to notice that she was wearing a thin nightgown, which she had shoved into her jeans for the trip outside, under her open coat. The fabric was worn enough so that he had no problem making out the shape of her breasts, including the tawny shade of her nipples.

Seth's heart was suddenly pounding in his ears and his body's response was intense and immediate. He met and held her gaze. He placed his gun on the end table and moved to her, hating himself for his own weakness.

Savannah's hair was mussed and her cheeks were stained a little scarlet from being out in the cold morning air. Her eyes were sultry, which seemed to intensify her disheveled appearance.

He saw the look of longing in her eyes, and that was all the encouragement he needed.

Placing his hands on either side of her small waist, Seth checked her expression again. Luckily, she showed no signs of resistance or repulsion. If anything, unspent passion filled her eyes. It nearly erased the blue, turning them a dark, imported chocolate color.

Beneath his hands, he could feel the quick, uneven breaths in her diaphragm. Slowly, he bent down and gave his first tentative touch of his lips to hers. It was sheer heaven.

Savannah surprised and pleased him when she placed her palms against his chest and stepped into his kiss. The feel of her hands against the mat of hair and his bare chest was almost enough to send him over an embarrassing edge.

She teased the seam of his lips with her tongue

until he opened his mouth. She tasted like mint, coffee and lust. Seth wrapped her in his arms, holding her against him as the kiss evolved from something tentative into a full-fledged erotic experience.

His fingers moved into her hair. He tilted her head gently, to gain better access to her sweet mouth. Again Savannah surprised and pleased him. She began to tease his nipples. Seth hadn't even considered his nipples an erogenous zone until that second.

He only wished that she was taller, then he might have had the exquisite pleasure of feeling her body pressed against his. Instead, he settled for forcing one leg between hers.

Savannah moaned softly into his mouth. He could actually feel her need and desire and it further pushed him toward a premature release. Something that hadn't occurred since his teens.

She slipped her hands around his naked torso as their lips remained locked together, their tongues exploring, testing and exciting. When her hands laced behind his head, Seth was treated to the feel of her breasts being pressed against his flesh.

He felt hard nipples and soft roundness.

Then he felt himself do the unimaginable.

His body wracked and convulsed against her hip. He was mortified.

But Savannah had a different reaction than what he

had expected. She deepened the kiss, turning it into something sweet and profound instead of passionate and needy. It was almost as if she was silently thanking him for being unable to control his own body.

"Oh, my heavens!"

Seth and Savannah jumped apart at the sound of Olive's voice. She was standing in the still-open doorway, holding a basket. Her expression was a blend of surprise and pleasure. Seth knew there was no way to gracefully explain why he was holding Savannah in the living room and he was sure he looked as guilty as Savannah did.

So far, this day was turning out to be a lot like his teen years. "I'm going to take a shower," he said, then made a hasty exit into the bedroom.

"Well, well," Olive said as she came in and started to unload freshly baked muffins. "I never would have put you together with Seth Landry."

"We're not together," Savannah insisted, mostly for herself.

Olive turned and gave her one of those yeah-right looks. Savannah relented slightly. "It was just one kiss," she promised her friend.

"One kiss?" Olive snorted. "I...um, watched for a moment before I made my presence known."

Savannah felt her cheeks heat with a blush at the mere thought that Olive had witnessed—what?

She placed a small jar of her homemade preserves on the counter. "And our sheriff has quite a body, doesn't he?"

Savannah's eyes grew wide. "Olive!"

"Well," the older woman said. "I may be old and crippled with arthritis, but I know a washboard stomach when I see it."

Despite her embarrassment, Savannah had to agree. The memory of feeling hard muscle beneath her palms was too fresh in her mind. As was the incredible intensity of the kiss itself. No man had ever kissed her like that. And certainly no man had ever shown her the depth of his desire in the way Seth had. For the first time in years, she felt both want and wanted.

Once she heard the shower running, Savannah gave a wicked smile to Olive. "Definitely has a great body."

Appearing pleased, Olive sat down in one of the kitchen chairs and asked for some coffee. Savannah poured cups for them both, then started a new pot before she joined Olive at the table.

Olive was the closest thing to a mother figure in her life, and Lord knew Savannah was feeling too many conflicting emotions. She needed a sounding board. "I think I'm losing my mind," she admitted to Olive.

"Why?"

Savannah took a fortifying breath. "Seth and me? There can't be a future in that."

"Why not?" Olive asked sincerely. "He's handsome, smart, and he's a *Landry*. Seems to me the only problem you have is keeping Ruthie Nestor away from him."

Savannah's heart plummeted into her stomach. "He's dating Ruthie?"

Olive gave and emphatic shake of her head. "No, Ruthie has had her hopes set on Seth since they were in high school together. As far as I know, that hasn't changed. Especially since Seth helps her out with that horrible child she has."

"Cal?"

"Cal the criminal," Olive corrected. "I had to ban him from the shop because he steals as easily as he breathes." Olive took a sip of her coffee. "But I don't want to talk about Cal. The topic is Seth."

Savannah raked her hands through her hair. "Olive, the man makes me weak in the knees, which is ridiculous since he's accused me of three murders."

Waving her hand dismissively, Olive said, "*That* was him just doing his job. What I saw a little bit ago had nothing to do with work."

"I've never felt this kind of instant attraction to a man," Savannah admitted.

"Ever hear of love at first sight?" Olive asked.

"Of course. But I never thought it was true."

"Until now?"

Savannah nodded, if cautiously. "Is it possible

that I've fallen in love with Seth in a matter of days?"

"Anything is possible," Olive reminded her.

"Did you know when you met your husband that he was the one?"

Olive's eyes clouded, as they always did whenever anyone mentioned her long-deceased husband. Savannah thought she must have loved him very much to still feel the pain of his loss. And she had never remarried in all this time. That had to mean she still felt married to a ghost. It was kind of sad and romantic in a weird way.

"We got married two weeks after we met," Olive said.

"Wow." Savannah was impressed. It also explained why Olive was such a terminal matchmaker. Obviously she believed in love, especially at first sight. "Then I guess it means it is possible for me to have feelings for Seth."

"Feelings? Darling, I've known you since the second day you arrived in Jasper. You're all work and school. It's good to see that Seth has cracked your practical shell. In fact, I think it's great!" Olive proclaimed excitedly. "We'll have a wedding shower and—"

"Slow down," Savannah insisted. "We were kissing, not getting engaged. Besides, I have no idea how Seth feels. He may have kissed me because I was convenient."

"Pooh," Olive huffed. "Men are very transparent at times. I've seen the way he looks at you. The man's in love."

Savannah swallowed the yelp of cheer that was her first response. "Maybe the man's just in lust," she pointed out. "Sometimes you can't tell the difference. Besides, even if he is in love, there's no future for us."

"Why would you say that?" Olive asked. "When you get your degree, you'll probably be working closely with Seth on cases and things."

*If I'm still here.* "Maybe," Savannah hedged.

"Well," Olive began as she rose, "you two enjoy the muffins." Olive smiled, knowingly. "*And* each other." Then she headed for the door. "I'll see you around one."

"Okay," Savannah called. "Thanks for talking to me, Olive."

The woman glanced over her shoulder, her eyes moist. "You know I think of you like a daughter. I just want you to know I'm always here for you."

"I know, and thanks."

Savannah pondered the complexities of her situation with Seth until she heard the shower stop. Then she went into Plan B mode—pretend it didn't happen unless he brings it up.

"NO MORE SCHOOL and no more Olive's." Seth proclaimed several hours later when she came out of the bedroom where she had been hiding.

She glared at him. "Wrong. I'm going to work and I'm going to school."

Seth's scowl was fierce and she noticed that his fists were balled at his sides. "How am I supposed to protect you when you're out in public?"

"I've been out in public since I got here," she reminded him. "The only thing that has changed is that now you know I'm a federally protected witness."

He took a threatening step closer. "You think that's the only thing that's changed?" His tone was low and almost threatening.

Much to her chagrin, Savannah had to crane her neck to maintain eye contact. Or more accurately, their glaring battle.

"Let's get *that* out of the way then."

"Out of the way?" he repeated sarcastically.

Savannah took a step back. She needed space to be able to do this. For some reason it was impossible for her to control her hormones when she could smell his cologne. "We kissed, Seth. Period. It won't happen again."

"Wanna bet?" he challenged.

She implored him with her eyes. "I should have said it *can't* happen again."

"Why?"

She rolled her eyes. "Because the government could yank me out of Jasper tomorrow. I know what it's like to leave behind people you love." The instant the words fell out of her mouth, Savannah wanted to die.

Seth didn't miss her little slip. "You love me?" His expression was now gentle, inviting and almost vulnerable.

"It wouldn't matter if I did," she insisted.

"It would to me."

Closing her eyes and dropping her head, she said, "I don't know. I only know that I've never felt like this about a man. It scares me."

Seth pulled her into his arms. It was the most comfortable place on earth. Softly, he stroked her hair. She could feel solid muscle and immediately her mind returned to when she had explored the impressive contours of his torso. *Lord, why can't I keep my mind out of the gutter!*

"If it makes you feel any better, I'm off balance, too."

"What does 'off balance' mean?" she asked as she placed her cheek so that she could feel the uneven beat of his heart.

"I think it means I'm falling in love with you."

Savannah stepped out of his arms and placed a finger to his lips. "*Don't* say that," she begged, feeling as if she wanted to burst into tears.

"Even if it's true?" he asked, the annoyance clear in his voice.

"You told me how hurt you were when your parents left you. Seth, the only difference between that situation and this one is that I *know* I'm going to be relocated again. I know I'll have to leave you one day." Savannah felt her eyes fill with tears, but she refused to allow herself to cry.

"You don't *know* that," Seth insisted.

"Look, Peter let Cody overrule him, but it won't be long before someone in the Justice Department hears I'm still in a possibly compromised city and yanks me out of here."

"You don't have to go," Seth said. "I can protect you."

"Protect me?" she parroted. "This morning you almost shot me because I went out for firewood."

"Excuse me!" Seth retorted. "I wake up and find you gone and the door standing open. What was I supposed to do?"

Realizing this was getting them nowhere fast, Savannah said, "Okay, so you were protecting me."

"Thank you." He didn't sound all that sincere. "Now, back to this idiotic notion of yours that you continue to live as if nothing has changed."

"It isn't idiotic," Savannah assured him through clenched teeth. "I'm going to work, then to class. This isn't open for discussion."

"Is that one of your favorite expressions?" Seth countered.

"When I'm dealing with someone who is being a hardheaded jerk, yes."

"Jerk?" he asked, though there was a tinge of amusement in his tone and one of his eyebrows arched questioningly. "The last person who called me a jerk got punched."

"I wouldn't suggest that," Savannah said. "I'm not one of your prisoners who you can punch when no one is looking."

"I wouldn't punch someone in custody," Seth assured her. "Shane called me a jerk, so I had no choice but to hit him."

Savannah shook her head. "That reminds me of home. My brothers pounded each other for any dumb reason."

"It wasn't a dumb reason. Anyway, I hit him, I didn't do any long-lasting harm. He had a bruise on his stomach for a while. End of injury."

"He had a bruise on his face in the photograph at your house. Was that also you?"

Seth shook his head. "Clayton."

Savannah raised her arms. "I'm sorry, I know you don't like to talk about him."

Seth shrugged. "It's no secret he's in prison for manslaughter because of Victoria DeSimone."

"Domestic violence?"

Seth shook his head and gave a melancholy laugh. "Nope, she was his paralegal and his lover. It was her testimony that put Clayton in prison. Perjured testimony, I might add."

"He's a lawyer? Can't you go to her and make her tell the truth?"

"He *was* a lawyer, and I can't find her. He was disbarred after the conviction almost a year ago. But Clayton has a hearing on a sentence reduction in a few months. We'll all be there to testify on his behalf."

"I hope it works," Savannah said. She meant it. It surprised her at how strongly she felt about this injustice toward the Landry family. It went beyond empathy for a friend. It went into dangerous ground. "Now, would you like to go to your office—" She was cut off by the telephone.

It was Cody and he wanted Seth. For some reason, it annoyed her that *her* marshal only wanted to talk to his brother. She felt out of the loop and didn't like it. At least the call only lasted a few seconds, so it couldn't have been too important.

"What did he want?" Savannah asked, silently telling herself that it was her house and her phone and she had every right to know because most importantly, it was her life.

"Don't panic," Seth said. "It wasn't a relocation order. Cody just wants to talk to me about some of the evidence from your date murders."

"I prefer if you didn't call them mine."

"Anyway, I told him to meet me at Olive's."

Savannah smiled. "Thank you."

He shrugged, then said, "I still think it's a lousy idea, but it's your life. And I do happen to agree that if someone wanted you dead, they would have killed you long ago."

"Thanks for that positive thought," she teased.

"C'mon," Seth said, taking her hand.

Savannah laced her fingers with his. It felt right. It felt natural.

But it was only temporary.

# Chapter Nine

Like most of the shops in Jasper, things were quiet at Olive's on Thursdays. Seth knew it was because the tourists from the nearby ski resorts were getting in the last runs of their vacations. So when he dropped Savannah at Olive's shop he wasn't surprised when Junior and Olive invited Savannah upstairs. She agreed to go up to the living quarters for some tea. He wondered if Savannah had only agreed because she knew Cody was coming by and she didn't want to risk letting Olive or Junior overhear the truth. He knew she regarded both of them as friends. At least Junior seemed thrilled that she was going upstairs. Though he claimed it simply gave him a break from doing the year-end figures for his mother, Seth sensed that Junior was smitten with Savannah. He didn't like the way that made him feel, though he did like the fact that Savannah seemed to treat Junior more like a big brother than Seth's potential romantic rival.

"I haven't even said anything and you're already frowning," Cody commented as he entered the shop.

"I wasn't frowning about you, and keep your voice down. Savannah is upstairs with the Baumgartners."

Cody smiled knowingly. "And you don't like Savannah giving attention to anyone but you?"

Seth's only response was a threatening glare.

Cody lifted his arms in mock surrender. "Look, I'm not blind. She's beautiful but she's a protected witness, Seth. You've gotta control whatever you're feeling. We don't even have a trial date and I can't promise you she'll be able to stay—"

"—in Jasper until then," Seth finished, irritably. "She's already given me this lecture."

Cody appeared relieved. "Good. I wouldn't want to see the two of you get involved and you be hurt."

"Too late," Seth admitted.

Cody looked at him in disbelief. "You seduced her the very first night you were supposed to be protecting her?"

"No, we just kissed."

"Well," Cody sighed, his annoyance clear.

"Promise me no more mouth-to-mouth incidents. I put my butt in a sling to convince my superiors that you were in complete control of the situation. Speaking of which, why is she working?"

"Because that wasn't open to discussion," Seth mimicked.

Cody whistled softly. "She can be a major pain," he commented. "She doesn't seem to want to follow the rules."

"Maybe she doesn't like your rules," Seth said.

"They're for her own protection," Cody answered, defensively.

"They're stifling to a woman like Savannah," Seth explained. "She would wither away stuck in that cabin with nothing to do."

"That *was* precisely what she was supposed to do," Cody countered. "I've got to keep her alive to testify."

"No, *I* have to do that. Savannah is my responsibility now."

"Not if you can't be objective and at the top of your game," Cody argued. "I need you to be one hundred percent on this thing."

"I'm at 110 percent now. Don't worry. I'll take good care of her."

"Make sure that's the only thing you take from her."

"I'm getting tired of this discussion," Seth said pointedly. "Didn't you want to tell me some things about the evidence?"

Cody nodded as they both leaned against the counter near the register, their heads together. "Harvey Whitlock's prints came back as one Harve Beagle, a minor-leaguer in the Rossi family."

Seth muffled a curse.

"It gets better," Cody insisted. "The guy who found Fowler's body, Ken Updyke, is also a grunt in the Rossi family."

"Damn," Seth whispered softly. "Rossi sent two hitmen here to kill her?"

"Our guy on the inside says no," Cody explained. "But he isn't privileged to everything."

"If Updyke and Whitlock were hitmen, how come they didn't hit Savannah? Why kill her dates?"

"Maybe they were two wimps who couldn't kill a woman. Or maybe they wanted to get her arrested for murder to eliminate her effectiveness as a witness when the Rossi racketeering trial starts."

"Any idea when that is?" Seth asked.

"Nope. That's Peter's department. He's the DOJ head of the investigation."

"He's had six years," Seth said with disgust.

"These things take time," Cody insisted. "Oh, by the way, I think I know what the 9-1-2 on Fowler's hand meant."

"What?"

"It was probably meant as a warning to Savannah."

"What kind of warning is 9-1-2?" Seth queried.

"It's the area code for Savannah, Georgia. I guess they just wanted to make their presence known."

"Well, they were pretty stupid. Apparently Savannah has no idea that is the area code. I asked her about the number and she thought Fowler had simply noted the time she had arrived for their date. He wasn't too thrilled that she was a few minutes late."

"Well, I'm still checking on the contract the Rossi family put out on her. I'll let you know what I find out. And oh, by the way, your killer likes trophies? Well, I think you're looking for a Glock 9mm. Apparently Harve never left home without it and it wasn't on your inventory."

"Great. If the killer somehow lost the Glock in the vent, then there's a possibility Cal found it."

"Cal the teenage criminal?" Cody asked.

"He was caught in the ventilation system after we had finished with the crime scene. At the time we didn't know the ventilation system was such an easy way in and out of the Mountainview. When I sent J.D. back, he learned that a bellman had caught Cal. So, I guess I'd better go track the kid down and see if he has the gun." Seth rubbed his eyes, hoping for Ruthie's sake that Cal hadn't already used the weapon in a felony. If so, there was nothing within his power to help the boy. He'd be on the fast bus to the reformatory, then on to an adult prison when he was of age.

Cody left, and Seth grumbled, "Dammit!"

"What?" Savannah asked as she came up behind him. "Did Cody bring bad news?"

He turned in her direction and Savannah was again amazed that just seeing his handsome face was enough to make her knees buckle.

He explained about Harvey Whitlock being Harve Beagle and Ken Updyke being his partner in the Rossi crime family. Savannah felt fear knot her stomach.

"But Cody can't find anything to indicate they were doing it on the orders of Rossi. Some agency has an operative undercover on the inside of Rossi's organization and he doesn't know anything about two lightweights like Whitlock and Updyke being sent by Rossi."

"Is that good or bad?"

He reached out and stroked the hollow of her cheek with the back of his hand. He had a fierce need to comfort her and he would have preferred pulling her into an embrace but didn't dare risk a repeat performance in front of gossip-mongering Olive or smitten Junior.

"Good. Especially since someone killed Whitlock. In my opinion, this is about making you look like a killer to destroy your credibility on the stand. Updyke probably killed Whitlock when you weren't arrested after the first murder."

"Sounds like the kind of friend I wouldn't want

to have," Savannah said honestly. "What about the trophies?" she asked.

"My guess is we'll eventually find them some-place you have access to. Well, all except for one."

"Whitlock's?"

Seth nodded. "We have to go see Cal Nestor right away. Can you leave?"

She nodded. "It's pretty slow, but I'm sure Olive won't mind. I mean, she's sitting up there with Junior, going over her books. She'll probably love an excuse to come down and man the shop. But what's the urgency?"

He told her about the gun. "My guess is Cal cut school today and is either off shooting it someplace, or he's trying to find a convenience store to rob."

"Then you're right, I suppose we had better hurry. Let me just run up and tell Olive I'm leaving."

While she was gone, Seth called the school and verified that Cal was on their absentee list. His second call was to the Cowboy Café, where he knew Ruthie would be working her usual double shift.

"Hello, handsome, what do you want sent to your office?"

"I'm calling about Cal," he said.

There was a brief, pained silence before she asked, "What did he do this time?"

"Hopefully nothing," Seth tried assuring her. "But I need to find him and he isn't in school."

"He isn't?"

"No. Where does he normally go when he skips school?"

"He likes to go to Clancy. He takes his horse and goes to the wildlife area there."

"Thanks, Ruthie."

"Thank you," she said in earnest. "I guess I'll have to come over and cook you a meal to show my gratitude."

"That's not necessary. I'm just doing my job."

In a sultry voice, Ruthie asked, "Seth Landry, are you telling me you don't want me to come over to quench all your…*appetites?*"

"Now's not a good time," he said, not wanting to hurt her. "I'll let you know how things work out with Cal."

"Thanks," Ruthie said with little enthusiasm, then she hung up.

Savannah was back quickly and they headed out to his Bronco. "Can you ride?" he asked.

"A horse?"

"No, a skateboard," he joked. "This is Montana, of course I meant a horse."

She playfully offered him her tongue. "I can probably ride better than you can. My father put me on a horse when I was four."

"I was just a matter of months old, so I think I have you beat."

"Really," she fairly purred. "Care to make a wager on that?"

"I hate to take your money."

"I'll be taking yours and I won't feel the least bit guilty about it."

"Okay. Just remember, this was your idea."

"Fine…say, a hundred dollars?"

"You're on."


SAVANNAH'S FIRST reaction to the Lucky 7 Ranch was a sense of awe. A huge clapboard home almost rivaled the beautiful peaks off in the distance. She saw miles and miles of fencing, and a corral off to the left side.

"This is like the western version of the Kennedy Compound, right?"

Seth chuckled. "It's a little large, but we needed all the space growing up. My father built this house with his own two hands."

"You're kidding," Savannah said as she climbed the stairs to the large double doors.

"Nope. Jasper is actually named for my great-great-grandfather. Jasper Landry claimed over two million acres when he arrived before Montana even thought about being a state."

"Wow."

"The land has been divided between family members, but the only two Landry spreads left are the Lucky 7 and Cade's ranch."

"Cade's married to the pretty redhead who had the premature baby boy, right?" Savannah asked.

"Jackson, and he's doing fine. Her name is Barbara. You should get to know her. She's another East Coast girl. Came here all the way from Charleston."

"My ears are burning!" he heard the unmistakable sound of Barbara's voice from the direction of the kitchen.

He led Savannah to the back of the house and found his sister-in-law, Callie, having milk with Cade's wife Barbara. "Is this a convention of the Landry mothers and mothers-to-be?" he asked as he bent and kissed them both on the cheek.

"That's Prather-Landry," Barbara retorted with a smile.

"Whatever," Seth said. "Barbara, I think you've met—"

"You're from Olive's Attic," Barbara interrupted. "I spend a fortune on vintage jewelry there. You've helped me a couple of times, right?"

Savannah nodded. "Yes. I'm Savannah and I'm here to take Seth's money."

Callie and Barbara smiled instantly.

"She's mistaken," he promised his relatives. "She bet me a hundred bucks that she was a better rider than I am."

"Maybe she is," Barbara opined, then to Savannah she said, "You go, girl. There's nothing better than seeing a Landry put in his place by a woman."

"Have you always hated men?" Seth teased with a smile.

"Yep. Except for Cade."

Seth chuckled, knowing full well that Barbara was just pulling his chain. Though she still commuted back to Charleston for business, it had evolved from the half-week schedule when she and Cade were first married to maybe twice a month. Seth knew Cade secretly wished she would stop her traveling. He missed Jackson when she took him to Charleston almost as much as he missed his wife. It was so bad that they had gone back to Cade flying her to and from Charleston in his Piper. For a while, Barbara had insisted on taking commercial flights so that Cade could get his work done.

Seth smiled. In many ways, Savannah was like Barbara. Both women definitely had minds of their own. That both earned his respect and infuriated him. At least it did with Savannah.

"Callie?" Seth asked. "Can Savannah borrow your parka? It's pretty bitter out there. Oh, and some gloves. She doesn't own any gloves."

Callie hoisted her very pregnant body out of the chair and said, "Sure. It isn't like I could zip the thing over this stomach. Whenever we go out, I about freeze. Unless I use one of Sam's coats, then I just have to roll the sleeves up about a foot."

Callie came back with the parka and a pair of well-insulated riding gloves. Savannah removed her coat and placed it on the back of a chair. Seth held the parka for her, carefully guiding her arms into the slightly bulky garment. It fit, sort of. It was a little big in the body, but at least he knew it would keep her warm during their ride to the wildlife preserve.

"How many pairs of socks do you have on?" Barbara asked.

"One," Savannah answered.

Barbara laughed. "You must be from a normal climate, too."

Savannah returned the smile. It was so natural that Seth felt a jolt through his whole system.

"I'll run up and get you another pair," Callie said.

"No stairs," Seth warned. "I'll go."

"Minimal stairs," Callie returned. "And I don't want you to go through my underwear drawer."

Seth rolled his eyes. "I have seen women's underwear before."

That earned him humorous looks from Barbara and Callie, but he got a different response from Savannah. A slight blush stained her cheeks, which was unfortunate given their present company.

"She's blushing," Barbara announced as she stood. "Geez, Seth, did you seduce her before or after you had her spend a night in your jail?"

Callie piped up with, "Please tell me it wasn't the night she was *in* your jail. If it was, I will no longer like you and you won't be the godfather of my baby."

"We haven't had sex!" Seth fairly screamed.

"Is that good or bad?" Taylor Reese asked when she appeared in the doorway with a full laundry basket. "Hi, Savannah. Ready for tonight's test?"

To his surprise, Savannah answered, "Yes. I got up at 4:00 a.m. and went over all my notes. There's nothing about victimology I don't know."

"I haven't even started yet," Taylor admitted. "I do better if I go over things right before they happen. Speaking of happenings, why is Seth yelling that you aren't having sex?"

*This is getting out of control!* Seth went to Taylor and had her fish a pair of heavy socks out of the neatly folded laundry. "Put these on while I change my shirt and get my riding boots," Seth advised Savannah. "And don't talk to any of them. They'll twist your words. Trust me."

"He's testy," Barbara said as soon as Seth had gone upstairs.

Savannah remained quiet, not because of Seth's warning, but because she didn't know how to respond to that.

"Sexual frustration," Taylor offered.

"I agree," Callie added. "Sam was like that before we got together."

"Cade, too," Barbara chimed in. "Landry men get very, very ill-tempered when they aren't getting any."

"Gee, Barbara," Seth said when he returned holding his coat and hopping on one foot to pull on the other boot. "Can you be a little more crass, I don't think Savannah has quite gotten the whole picture yet."

Barbara made a dismissive noise very much like a grunt. "You know it's true, Seth Landry. Or do you expect us to believe that you see Ruthie every couple of weeks just for a home cooked meal? Face it, Landry men just have *needs*. It's as hereditary as the sexy half smile you all have."

"Shane doesn't have it," Taylor said. "He only has outdated come-ons."

"For the zillionth time, Ruthie and I are just good friends," Seth said, "Let's go, Savannah."

She was more than willing to comply. The conversation was a tad frank for her. Actually, that wasn't true. What was bothering her was thinking about Seth having a sex partner.

Snow crunched beneath her feet as she walked in silence next to Seth.

"Don't brood," he warned.

"I'm not brooding, I'm thinking."

"About Ruthie Nestor and me?"

"Yes. I feel uncomfortable knowing I kissed you when you have—"

"What I have with Ruthie is a friendship. I look after her son. She appreciates that. Yes, we tried dating a few years back, but it didn't work. We parted as mutual friends, in spite of what most of greater Jasper seems to think."

Savannah remained silent.

Seth grasped her arm and forced her to look at him. "Listen. Ruthie isn't an issue. Got it?"

"Okay," Savannah said as she pulled her arm free. "I no longer feel like a poacher."

"Poacher?" he repeated, incredulous. "I can promise you, Savannah. I've never felt this way before about any woman. I know you don't want to hear this but I lo—"

Quickly, she covered his mouth with her gloved hand. "Don't. Don't even think it." She took her hand away.

Seth appeared so frustrated she guessed he would love to punch something. Still, she had to stick to her guns. Falling in love was not allowed. *So why did the mere thought make her want to cry?*

She was given her choice of horses and Savannah decided on a gray mare who seemed to have some life in her.

"You sure?" Seth asked.

"Yes, why?"

"Because Betsy is a little skittish."

Savannah grinned up at him. "I'm very good at calming animals."

"Just remember, she was your choice," Seth warned. "Especially when you have to cough up a hundred bucks."

One of the hands, a man called Bull, saddled and readied the horses for them. Well, truthfully, Seth saddled his horse and Bull saddled hers.

Ignoring the hand Seth offered to help her mount, she managed to get her foot in the stirrup and sit the saddle without his aid. She gave him a saccharin smile once she had accomplished the task without assistance.

Seth was grumbling something about hardheadedness as he went over and lithely swung his large frame onto the animal.

The gray was skittish, as Seth had warned. No amount of petting and soothing her seemed to control her nervousness. Still, Savannah was sure the horse would come through for her once they were on their way. Because of the deep snow, Seth and Savannah had to ride first on paths already cleared on the property, then out onto the highway. So far, she was controlling her skittish animal as well as he was handling his expertly trained stallion.

"I'm winning," she announced as she pulled up on the inside.

"How do you figure that?" he scoffed.

"My horse is much more difficult to manage, so I'm obviously the better rider."

"The trip isn't over yet," he said.

Savannah had forgotten how much she loved riding. She'd been going at least a couple times a week since she moved to Jasper, thanks to a local stable that rented to tourists. But this was the first time she was able to ride freely in the shadows of the Rockies.

They were so majestic, they nearly took her breath away. The only thing she could think of that was more attractive was the man next to her. *Stop it!* her brain screamed.

Soon they entered the wildlife reserve in Clancy. There were paths, so Seth led her to one that placed them beneath snow-ladened pines. It was pure magic to be in such an incredible place. She could smell the fresh mountain air and feel it cool her lungs. Everywhere she looked, she saw pristine forest and the occasional hint of a stream winding through the park.

They had been riding less than fifteen minutes when Savannah heard pops that sounded like firecrackers. Apparently so did her horse, because Betsy became jittery again.

"Do they do that to move the animals from one part of the refuge to another?" she asked.

"Nope, if my hunch is correct, that's Cal Nestor shooting a gun he found in the ventilation system. I think the killer dropped his trophy in his haste to climb out and Cal is currently using it to shoot at something."

"Or someone," Savannah mumbled. The thrill of competition drained away and was replaced by real, genuine fear.

## Chapter Ten

"Or," Savannah began tentatively, "it isn't Cal. It's some kind of poacher. If so, shouldn't we call the wildlife police, or whatever they're called?"

"If it's a poacher—which I'm pretty sure it isn't—I'll handle it."

He spoke with such authority that Savannah truly believed him. She also remembered that he had a gun on him somewhere. That made her feel a tad safer.

They continued to ride, getting closer to the sporadic sounds of the shooting. The closer they got, the more anxious her horse became. Savannah empathized. She wasn't exactly used to going *in the* direction of gunfire. In New York, there'd been a shooting on her block. She had raced around the corner as if her life depended upon it. Actually it had, since the shooters turned out to be two romantic rivals firing wildly at each other in the middle of a normally quiet street.

Seth held out a hand indicating she should stop. Looking ahead about ten yards or so, Savannah saw a tall, gangly teenager with carrot-colored hair standing in a rocky clearing with a brown mare tethered nearby. He was standing with his back to them. On the edge of a large bolder about ten feet in front of him were rows of several soda cans.

Seth dismounted and handed her the reins to his horse. She watched in amazement as Seth soundlessly managed to cross the snowy path, until he was within a foot of the kid.

"Hi, Cal," Seth said calmly, as if he were there to discuss the scenery.

Cal turned, his freckled face shocked, then filled with the defiance only a teenager can display. "What are you doing here?" he challenged.

Savannah could tell by his body language that the boy wasn't at all as brave as his voice. He was shifting from foot to foot and kept one hand behind his back. She already knew that the one hand held the gun Seth hoped would help solve Whitlock's murder, which might solve the other two, as well. Which would mean she would no longer be the topic of the gossip hounds and she'd have evidence that might spur Peter into action. Surely adding murder charges would make him schedule the trial sooner. *Right?*

Lifting his coat, Seth reached into the back waistband of his jeans and retrieved his gun. Cal's eyes seemed to grow as wide as one of those Precious Moments children.

"You can't shoot me for ditching school," Cal insisted.

"I'm not going to shoot you," Seth said reasonably.

Seth proceeded to shoot each of the cans in turn, knocking them off the boulder. Savannah was impressed and for a second, she saw that Cal was, too. Then he donned his mask of attitude again.

Savannah didn't hear what happened next. Her spooked horse suddenly reared up while Savannah was trying to hold the reins of Seth's horse, as well.

"Hang on, girl," she soothed as she did everything in her power to get the skittish horse mellowed out.

Seth appeared by her ride, saying, "Having troubles, great rider?"

"Take these," she snapped, tossing the reins at him with no care where they hit him. "Woah, girl," she soothed as the horse reared again.

"Need some help?" Seth asked.

"No," she assured him. It took her a few minutes and a lot of cajoling to get the animal to stop rearing and bucking. All the while, Savannah deftly used her thighs to stay in the saddle. Heck, she would have used her tongue if it meant staying on the animal. She was not going to give Seth the satisfaction of getting the better of her on a bet.

"Okay," Seth said, once she had the animal under control. "I owe you a hundred bucks."

She looked at him questioningly, confused that he would acquiesce before the ride home.

Seth offered a guilty but attractive half smile. "Betsy there isn't known for her comfort around loud noises," he explained. "Which is why I tried to get you to pick another horse before we left. I figured she would bolt when she heard the gunshots."

Savannah was angry. "You could have gotten me killed!"

Seth mounted his horse. "I don't think so. She's never been quite that aggressive before. I had no idea she'd buck, but you seem to have everything under control."

"Gee, thanks."

Seth chuckled. "If she had thrown you, you'd have landed in the soft snow. The only thing I figured you'd hurt was your pride."

"You are such a gentleman," Savannah returned, each syllable dripping with sarcasm. She looked up into the open space where Seth and Cal had been. The boy wasn't there. "What did you do to Cal?" she demanded.

"I made him climb down and pick up the cans I shot. It was either that or a fifty-dollar fine. I made it his choice."

Savannah had to admit that was pretty good manipulation. "You're an incredible shot. Did he have the gun?"

Seth patted his jacket pocket. "Thanks. It's important for a law enforcement officer to be a good shot. And the Glock is right here."

"You're more than a good shot. You're exceptional." Savannah felt herself truly relax for the first time in a while. "That's great. You can get fingerprints and find out who is doing this to me, right?"

"Thank you again and maybe," Seth said. They turned and started back for the ranch. "Depends if Cal smudged all the usable prints."

"Don't even *think* that," Savannah insisted. "I want this over with as soon as possible."

"I'll handle it as expeditiously as possible. I'm going to have J.D drive it to the lab today."

"Can you light the same fire under Peter White? I want this trial behind me so I can go back to my real life in Connecticut."

"Connecticut, huh?" Seth made it sound like a vile curse.

"Of course. That's where my family is. My roots, just like you're rooted to Jasper."

His jaw was taut when he asked, "You really couldn't stand living here permanently?"

Savannah felt tremendous guilt. "Seth," she began softly, "we've been over this. Even after the trial, if there's still a contract out on me, I'll have to remain in the Witness Protection Program. I can't think of anything in terms of permanency. It wouldn't be fair."

"To which one of us?" Seth countered, clearly angry.

"Me. You. Both of us, I guess."

He turned and held her gaze. "Has it dawned on you that I'd be happy for whatever time we could be together? I know you can't make promises, but I'd rather have one day with you than a lifetime with any other woman."

Savannah truly wanted to cry. "I don't think I can do that, Seth. I'm sure you could tell this morning that it's been more than six years since I've been held or kissed like that. I don't want a one-night thing with you. I need all or nothing. Because of my situation, it has to be nothing."

She turned to his strong, handsome profile. Seth was glaring straight ahead. "Seth?"

He wouldn't look at her. She tried calling his name again. Still nothing.

"Be childish," she snapped. "Just respect my feelings and my decision. This topic is no longer open for discussion."

Seth pulled his horse to an instant halt, grabbed her reins in the process. He looked deep into her eyes and said, "This topic is still open for discussion. I'll bring it up anytime I want because I think you're lying to both of us."

"I am not!"

"Do you want me to drag you off that horse and kiss you again?" he taunted. "And don't try telling me that this morning was just about some long dry spell you've had. I felt your desire, Savannah. I felt the way you pressed yourself against me, but mostly I felt the emotion behind your kiss."

"I never said I didn't find you attractive," she lamely claimed.

"Tell yourself whatever you need to," Seth said. "Just remember that I don't intend to follow your rules."

"Meaning?"

"Meaning that when I think you're ready, I'm going to make love to you."

SAVANNAH WAS HAVING a very difficult time concentrating on her test notes, thanks to Seth's earlier warning. Well, she would just have to make sure she never appeared ready and willing to the arrogant man.

She was seated in his Bronco outside the sheriff's office under the watchful eye of Deputy Greg. She was supposed to be reviewing her notes, but she couldn't seem to hold on to any of the information she'd been reading. Darn him for disrupting her life!

Seth returned shortly, followed by J.D., who was carrying the Glock in an evidence bag. Seth got in the car after speaking to Greg. J.D. was already speeding off somewhere with his sirens and lights blaring.

She checked her watch when he got in the car and started the engine. "I'm going to be late," she told him curtly.

"No, you won't," he assured her. Then he turned on the sirens and lights on top of the Bronco and headed toward Montana West University.

"Isn't this some sort of abuse of power?" she asked.

"Nope. It's getting you to class on time. How long is your class?"

"Normally it's three hours." She saw the pained look on his face. "But it shouldn't take me more than forty minutes to take the exam."

He gave her a quick glance. "Don't rush through it on my account."

"I'm not," she said. "Tests are normally the easiest part of a course for me."

"Brains and beauty," Seth said.

Savannah's heart fluttered slightly at the compliment. "Thank you."

"Oh, so now you're being formal with me? Care to tell me why?"

"Because of what you said earlier at the wildlife refuge. I don't want to say anything to give you the impression—"

"Savannah, you don't have to say anything. I'll know by looking into your eyes. They are the windows to your soul."

"My soul feels the same way my intellect does," she insisted.

"I warned you not to test me, Savannah," Seth said as he pulled the Bronco onto the shoulder and stopped. After releasing both their seat belts, he dragged her across the console and held her in his lap.

He took her mouth with such hungry pleasure that Savannah knew she was incapable of not showing a response. It was just too delicious an experience for her to pretend otherwise.

His mouth slowed, became gentler. Then he lifted his head and peered straight into her eyes. "You want this as much as I do, don't you?"

She didn't answer. She didn't have an answer, she just knew she wanted to feel his mouth on hers again. Lifting her hand to his head, she pulled him back down to her. Instantly, he was coaxing her lips apart. Her breaths were coming in short gasps and her heart was pounding against her rib cage.

He effortlessly made her insides catch fire. He lifted his dark head long enough to unzip her coat. Slipping his hands inside, Seth touched her fluttering stomach, then moved higher, until his hand closed over one breast.

Savannah moaned and panicked all at the same

time. "Don't do this," she implored. "I'm not ready for this."

Seth moved his hand instantly, then gently returned her to her seat. His dark eyes were still filled with unspent passion when he said, "Your intellect just betrayed you."

She remained silent. What could she say? He was right. The minute he touched her she turned into a quivering blob of hormonal need. It was disheartening to realize that she was so transparent. It had never happened before. She'd suffered her way through more than one desperation date and several blind dates. The men never seemed to pick up on the fact that she would have rather removed her own spleen with an oyster fork than be out with them. *So how come some small town cowboy seems to know me better than I know myself?*

*Because he must realize that I'm in love with him. Lord, what a mess. How do I keep him from using it against me?*

"I can't," she muttered.

"What?" Seth asked.

She hesitated for a brief second, then said, "I can't seem to keep my information straight, thanks to you."

Seeing his pleased grin out of the corner of one eye didn't exactly make Savannah happy.

She was in a vile mood when she walked into her class a little while later. Thankfully, Seth agreed to wait in the student lounge across from her class-room. The last thing she needed was to have him sitting next to her while she tried to remember things like the use of victimology in profiling and all the elements that were supposed to be in the profile.

She gave Taylor a reassuring smile before they began the exam.

True to her word, Savannah was finished in less than thirty-five minutes. Molly Jameson, her profes-sor, took her blue exam booklet and didn't seem the least bit surprised that she'd finished so quickly. But this was her third class with Molly, so Molly was familiar with Savannah's fast recitation of facts and theories.

Molly mouthed the words "Good night," before Savannah walked out the door.

She entered the lounge at the exact moment Seth's pager began to beep furiously.

"You are quick," he remarked as he read the number. "It's my office," he told her. "Can we go now? I'll call from the car phone."

Savannah dug into her purse and produced a cell phone and passed it to him. "Government issue," she said kind of shyly.

"Are you allowed to let other people use it?"

"It's supposed to be used when I need help or in-formation. Maybe the call is from J.D. and they have the fingerprints back."

Seth shook his head as he punched in a number.

"It will take them a while to lift the prints off the Glock. I sent along Cal's and mine for elimination purposes, but—"

He stopped in midsentence, listening, then spoke into the phone. "You didn't recognize the voice?"

Then, "I'm on my way there."

Followed by a very loud, "I don't care, she'll just have to deal with it. Get me a warrant ready. I'll be there in less than an hour."

Seth handed the phone back to Savannah and excitedly said, "We either have a crank call or our first solid lead."

Her heart jumped and she felt joy. "What is it?"

## Chapter Eleven

"It's Angelica Seagal."

"The designer?" Savannah asked as they walked toward the Bronco. "Someone thinks Angelica is the killer? Isn't that a little far-fetched?"

"Maybe," Seth acknowledged. "But she does have Vincent working for her and according to Mable, Angelica has a gun so popular it has its own permit."

"A .22?"

Seth nodded as he unlocked the car. "We'll swing by so I can get the warrant, then pay a visit to Jasper's resident jewelry designer."

"Is she as weird as everyone says?"

"And then some," Seth assured her. "She's a recluse with a passion for Native American clothing, even though there are no Native Americans in her ancestry."

"She sounds eclectic."

"*That* she is."

"But why would she have killed the three men?" Savannah wondered aloud.

"Two men," Seth corrected. "I think we can safely assume that Ken Updyke killed his partner, Whitlock. Cody has every agency in the U.S. and Interpol looking for him as we speak."

"Okay, then why would Angelica, this famous designer, want to kill a man she's never met and the man who supplies her with her gems?"

"We'll know when we get there."

Seth drove like the proverbial bat out of hell. Even with the stop to pick up the search warrant and the inventory list of gems from Grayson's briefcase, they were pulling up to the locked gate at Angelica's massive home-studio in under an hour.

Seth pressed a small button on a speaker box. He got no response, even though they could clearly see lights on up at the house. Sam pressed again. Still nothing. He muttered a curse and turned on his sirens and lights.

Savannah could hear some muffled voice from the speaker box, but Seth apparently had no intention of turning off the siren and lights. His obstinacy paid off, and in a few seconds, the high electric gate began to swing open.

Probably to punish the temperamental artist, Seth didn't cut the lights and the siren until he shut off the engine in front of the house.

Angelica's house was landscaped and well lit on the outside. All the January snow had been removed from the large lawn and all the shrubs. She wondered what they had done with all that snow. Probably trucked it to Brock Creek. Or they had a freezer full of snowballs. It was a massive historic home, made to look even larger by the white paint on everything, including the doors and shutters. Apparently Angelica's artistic talents didn't include complimentary trim on shutters.

Still, it was incredible. The front portico even dwarfed Seth.

Vincent opened the door, scowling and looking so much like Lurch that Savannah couldn't think of him by any other name. He had to be close to seven feet tall, emaciated to the point where his cheeks fell into his face. His hair was snow-white, as were his eyebrows. His mouth was thin and appeared out of place on his otherwise large face.

Seth took out the warrant and pressed it into Lurch's concave chest. "This gives me the authority to search the premises."

"I'll have to check with Miss Seagal."

Seth muscled his way past Lurch, bringing

Savannah with him. "Check away. I'll start searching."

"You can't do that without permission from Miss
Seagal. She's in the middle of working on a piece.
Can't this wait until morning?"

"No." Seth was emphatic. "I'll give you about
three minutes to get Miss Seagal here. After that I
start searching without her being present."

*Lord, he even groaned like Lurch!* Savannah
thought as he shuffled off through what appeared to
be a dining area. Savannah used the opportunity to
wander over to the beautifully carved staircase.
Peering up, she realized the house was four levels,
and they all appeared to be the same sanitary white
as the exterior.

Only the pale oak floors added drab color to the
rooms. She never would have pegged this as the home
of a world-renowned jewelry designer. It looked more
like a hospital or sanitarium, and she told Seth as much.

"It is pretty creepy," he agreed. "I hope this lets
me off the hook for having had animals on my walls.
Which," he began as he moved closer, his lips just
a whisper from her ear, "I asked J.D. to swing by and
take down."

"What?" Savannah asked, shocked. "You took
down your tribute to roadkill? Why?"

His gaze held hers. "For you."

Savannah knew she shouldn't, she just couldn't
help it.

She smiled at the kind gesture. "But there's not much chance that I'll be back to your home."

"Yes, there is," he said. "Until we catch our killer, I think we should move around a bit. Stay at my place, out at the ranch, your house. Just want to keep the person on their toes."

Savannah pursed her lips. "I guess that means you don't think Angelica is our killer."

"I'm just planning ahead," he said.

A waft of perfume preceded Angelica Seagal. Instantly, the pure white Maltese she was holding yapped a couple of times, but she soothed the dog and continued to cradle him or her in her arms.

She was dressed in the same shade as the oak flooring. Some kind of buckskin dress and leggings completed by a pair of leather moccasins with a triangular bead design on the top.

Angelica's outfit was authentic, right down to the strap ties at her shoulders and a complete lack of undergarments. She was a full-figured woman, so it was hard to miss her heavy breasts swaying unchecked in the vicinity of her waist.

Savannah guessed she was at least sixty. Angelica made no attempts to hide that fact. Somehow, it didn't mesh with Samantha's understanding that Angelica had been Bill Grayson's prom date. Her hair was salt-and-pepper, parted in the center, and allowed to flow well past her shoulders. She had a good six inches of split ends and a very angry expression on her sun-weathered face. She didn't look like your typical killer.

"What do you mean by barging in here to search my home?" Then she turned her faded hazel eyes on Savannah and asked, "And why, pray tell, did you bring along a store clerk? This must be a violation of some law."

"Nope," Seth answered. "According to Judge Duckett, I have every right to search every inch of this place for the items listed on the warrant. Now, you can either show me where they are, or I can go on my own search."

Angelica's face turned even more sour as she glanced at the warrant. "Relating to the murders of Richard Fowler and Bill Grayson? You've got to be kidding."

"This is no joke, ma'am," Seth assured her.

"You want my gun and diamonds, rubies and emeralds?" she read. "I'll have Vincent go get you the gun."

"No," Seth said urgently. "I need to be the one to retrieve it. We need to preserve all the fingerprints. Speaking of which, I'll need you and Vincent to come by my office tomorrow to have your prints taken for exclusion purposes."

A slow, dark red stain spread from Angelica's wrinkled neck up to cover her entire face. "Young man, I can't possibly come to your office. I wasted two days this week finishing up my taxes and I have some special order pieces for some very important clients."

"With all do respect, ma'am, I don't care if you're making special pieces for the Queen. You'll be in my office before noon tomorrow or I'll send a deputy to bring you and Vincent in. Your choice."

Angelica handed Lurch the Maltese. He looked pretty foolish holding such a small dog with its hair pulled back in a nearly invisible white bow.

Savannah and Seth followed her up to the third floor. Angelica wasn't taking this well.

"I can tell you that I haven't fired my gun in years and I can account for every moment of my time. I keep very detailed journals for myself and Vincent."

Savannah was surprised to see a touch of color in Angelica's bedroom. There were a few framed photographs on a massive dressing table. There was also a collection of perfume atomizers. But that wasn't what she thought most interesting. There wasn't a speck of dust to be found. Even the eleven-foot ceilings—also painted pure white—seemed to be devoid of cobwebs. Lurch must be a very busy boy to keep a place this size so spotless.

Angelica opened a drawer in her French-style end table and was about to reach in when Seth clamped down on her wrist with a viselike grip. That seemed to panic Angelica. She leapt away from him the instant he let go.

While Seth carefully took the gun from the

drawer with a pen and placed it in a bag from the pocket of his leather jacket, Savannah silently evaluated Angelica. The woman appeared to have a full litany of psychological disorders. The compulsive need for cleanliness, an aversion to being touched, her ill ease around people, and the whole thing with the white. The list just kept getting longer and she knew Molly would have a field day diagnosing this woman. Whether she could be successfully treated was a whole other matter. Angelica didn't seem like the kind of person who would be open to getting professional help.

"The jewels?" Seth prompted.

"I don't have them," Angelica insisted. "So now you can leave? I'm not involved in any of this and I resent the intrusion."

Seth shook his dark head. The action caused several locks of his hair to fall forward and it was everything Savannah could do to keep from reaching out and brushing them back into place.

"Isn't *she* the one who killed those men?" Angelica fairly screamed as she pointed a slightly bent finger in Savannah's direction.

"Miss Wyatt has been cleared of all suspicion," Seth said.

Funny, but that was the first time he had actually said that aloud. It sounded wonderful.

"Was that before or after you became lovers?" Angelica spat. "It's all over town."

"We are *not* lovers," Savannah told the batty woman.

"And if we were, it wouldn't be anyone's business," Seth added.

Savannah felt her cheeks warm, and wished Seth hadn't left the possibility open.

"Well, why on earth would you think I had Bill's jewels? He was killed *before* we had an opportunity to meet and discuss prices."

"We received a tip," Seth said. "May I please see your studio now?"

Angelica let out a string of very unfeminine curses as she led them back down to the first floor and through the white dining room, complete with two white floral arrangements on the Chippendale table for twenty.

They traveled through a narrow hallway to a closed door, which Angelica opened. The scent of butane and metals was pretty thick, and this room was also white, but it wasn't spotless like the rest of the house. In fact, this wasn't even a regular room. Angelica had torn through the ceilings, so the area was four stories high with skylights and track lighting everywhere.

There were several workstations, and Savannah recognized a few things, like a polishing machine and a diamond blade cutter. The other items strewn around the cluttered, disordered room were completely foreign, but interesting.

Angelica took Seth over to the right-hand wall, where a cabinet about ten feet long by ten feet high stood. It appeared old, as if perhaps it had once been part of an apothecary shop. Or maybe it was left in the house from the beginning. This was the first assay office in Jasper, maybe the cabinet had something to do with assaying. Savannah was about as fluent in assay materials as she was in jewelry-making equipment and tools.

"That's not possible!" Angelica was screaming. "I had no idea those were there!"

Savannah watched as Seth slipped on a Latex glove and pulled a rather large bag of gems out of one of the higher drawers.

"Those aren't mine!" Angelica continued to protest.

Seth gave the woman a warning look, then said to Savannah, "Help me compare the inventory, please." He handed her a glove.

Angelica slumped onto a stool at one of the workstations while Seth and Savannah counted the stones. "This has to be some cruel joke, or maybe someone put them there to implicate me. But my journals will prove that neither Vincent nor I was anywhere near the Mountainview Inn when *her* dates were murdered."

There was the exact number of each kind of stone, but neither of them knew how to determine carat weight.

"Miss Seagal." Seth went to her and isolated one of the stones through the bag. "Is this a three-carat ruby?"

She nodded. Seth then went through the tedious job of having her estimate the weights and sizes without actually touching them or the bag.

Once he had sufficient confirmation, he pulled a pad out of the breast pocket of his shirt. "I'm giving you a receipt for the .22 and the gems," he explained to Angelica.

"I have no idea how those gems got here!" she insisted.

"Has anyone been in the house recently? A stranger, a repairman, anyone?"

She shook her head. "No."

Seth nodded and said, "Don't forget about coming to the office for fingerprints."

"Is that really necessary?" Angelica whined. "I've told you everything I know and I've given you my gun. I have no protection should someone break in."

"You have Vincent," Seth told her. "I'm serious, Miss Seagal. If you aren't there by noon tomorrow, I'll send a deputy for you."

"I don't think I like you," Angelica commented, slightly more angry after Seth's threat. To Savannah, she said, "And I'm *sure* I don't like you."

Savannah smiled. "The feeling is mutual. Have a nice evening, Angelica." Seth grabbed her hand and led her away.

Outside, Savannah turned to Seth. "She's crazy, Seth. Maybe she's paranoid enough to kill. She's a catalogue of personality disorders, one of which is a tendency to attack without provocation because of some perceived paranoia. Maybe one of her paranoias is men and she's driven to kill."

"Thanks for the profile, but my gut tells me it isn't either of them. In fact, I think the gems were planted," he said as they reached the Bronco.

"She cooperated, and I just can't see looney Angelica or Vincent shooting anyone and putting them in Brock Creek. Not to mention, how would they know to write 9-1-2 on Whitlock's hand?"

Savannah was blowing warm breath into her cold hands as she waited for Seth to start the engine and the heat to get going. It was close to midnight and the temperature couldn't be much above zero. Savannah yawned. It had been a long day. Not to mention alternatingly trying and exciting.

Apologetically, Seth said, "I have to log this stuff at the office. It won't take me but a minute."

"I'm fine," she assured him.

Seth gave her that sexy half smile and patted her leg. That was enough to make adrenaline replace fatigue. She battled to keep her pulse from quickening and her mind from wandering into forbidden territory. She lost the battle before they were out of Angelica's drive.

Luckily, Angelica's house was only two blocks

from Main Street, so Seth was able to keep his word about being quick. He left the Bronco running, and when he was once again behind the wheel, he turned back toward the highway. Only he was going in the wrong direction.

"Where are we going?"

"My place," he said. "It's closer and we're both exhausted."

"But I don't have anything with me to spend a night away from home!"

He smiled and brushed his knuckles against her cheek. "We'll go back to your place first thing in the morning so you can change. And I've got an extra toothbrush."

"In case someone should drop by? Then you'll have Ruthie *and* Savannah rumors to contend with."

"Are you embarrassed by the thought that the town will think we're…together?"

"When pigs fly. Is this really necessary?"

"Yes." Then he turned and winked at her before saying, "This topic is no longer open for discussion."

"Smart ass."

"And here I thought it was your favorite expression."

"It is," she assured him. "But only when *I'm* saying it!"

SETH'S HOUSE looked a little bare without the animal trophies, but she had to admit, she felt much more comfortable without the dead animals watching her with their eerie glass eyes.

"Want some wine?" Seth offered.

"That would be great." Maybe that will make me less nervous. *I hate the way being alone with him makes me feel like I'm standing on pins and needles.*

He returned with the wine, and guided her into the living room. It was a very masculine room with leather furniture and rustic accents like a boot stool and leather window treatments. He went to the fireplace, moved the screen, and started a fire. When he returned the screen, she realized that it had to be custom-made. It had the cowboy motif of the Lucky 7. Like her with her hatboxes, Seth had his own way of keeping something of his former home in his new one.

He joined her on the sofa, his dark features softened by the flicker of the flames. He looked so appealing at that moment that Savannah was sure she wanted to ask him to make love to her. Instead, she took a long sip of her wine.

He reached out, took her glass and set it on the table. Without warning, he lifted her into his arms. Savannah knew she should probably put up some sort of virginal struggle, but it wasn't in her. He carried her upstairs into his bedroom.

By the time they reached the bed, Savannah had wrapped her arms around his neck and was already feeling the thrill of anticipation.

Still, that little voice of reason inside her head was trying to be heard above the pounding of her heart.

"I haven't touched you since the car," Seth whispered as he laid her down. "I need to feel you again. I want you, Savannah."

Savannah's mouth went dry as she watched him remove his Stetson, then his shirt, before he joined her on the bed. *Geez, but the man had a body to die for!*

The way he was looking at her made her feel so wanted, so special. His expression and the feel of his taut muscles beneath her hands seemed to bring an electric current into the room with them.

Savannah's little voice was getting weaker and more distant.

This time, Seth kissed her and slipped his hand under the waistband of her sweater simultaneously. Savannah was near the delirious stage.

She was still being tormented by her conscience.

Seth was softly molding her breasts, bringing her nipples to complete erectness. His mouth left hers as he placed kisses on her cheek, her jawbone, her collarbone, then finally his mouth closed over her breast.

Savannah cried out from the sheer pleasure of it. All she could do was hold his head and arch her back toward the incredible sensations he was treating her to.

Seth lifted one leg over her, trapping her in place

as his hand slid down over her stomach. It tickled and delighted at the same time. Then his hand moved lower, until he was touching her most intimate area through the rough fabric of her jeans.

She felt her own desire surge through her, clearing her mind of everything but her need for Seth.

Then the little voice spoiled it.

The desire she was feeling suddenly turned into guilty pleasure. No matter how she felt about him or how much she wanted him, she couldn't do this.

Seth must have sensed her sudden change of heart. His hand stilled and he lifted his head, looking at her with eyes filled with dark, dangerous unspent passion. She braced herself for harsh words.

"I take it your conscience has kicked in?" he asked. Amazingly, his tone contained nothing more than disappointment. There was no recrimination, no anger.

Savannah rolled out from under the trapping of his leg and adjusted her bra and her sweater. Her body ached but not as much as her heart. She never wanted anything this much. But she couldn't have Seth on her terms. There would be no happily-ever-after for them.

Unable to look at him, Savannah mumbled a hurried apology and got off his bed. As she did, she felt herself step on something.

Reaching down, she lifted a small medal on a

chain. Somehow she didn't see Seth as the holy medal type, but it must have come off when he partially undressed. She tossed it to him. "Here, this must have come off."

Seth looked at it and his face suddenly became a mask of anger. "This is too strange. How would he know I'd bring you here?"

"Excuse me?"

"This is a Saint Barnabas medal. I believe it was taken off Fowler's dead body."

# Chapter Twelve

Savannah was still shaken the next day when Seth dropped her off at Olive's Attic. It had taken some arguing, but she was able to convince Seth that going to his office to look into the gems, the medal, the Glock and Angelica's .22 were far more important than standing around the shop while she waited on customers.

She was also pretty sure his agreement had little to do with her argument, but more to do with the knowledge that the killer had been inside his house. Now it was more personal to him. She definitely knew the feeling.

J.D. was dispatched to check for signs of forced

entry and to dust all the doors and windows for prints. Deputy Greg got the great assignment of sitting in his personal pickup in front of Olive's shop. Apparently, he was her sitter until Seth came back.

"What gives?" Olive asked as she came down the stairs using her cane.

"I've sold three dresses, five sets of earrings and that ugly wagon the Kings gave us on consignment."

"That's great!" Olive said. "But I was referring to the fact that we have a deputy parked out front."

Savannah hated lying to a friend. "I've had a few problems with a guy from school. Deputy Greg is Seth's idea."

Olive's expression brightened. "Seth is watching out for you? Sounds like it's getting serious."

"It is not getting serious. It's getting complicated."

"Same thing. I'm just sorry Junior isn't here. He seemed quite pleased when I told him about you and Seth."

"Olive! Please don't tell people. For all I know this could be just a passing phase. You know, two lonely people in the right place at the wrong time?"

Placing her hand on her hip, Olive's brow furrowed. "You aren't making any sense, girl. Seth Landry is the catch of all catches. He's gorgeous, intelligent and rich. What more could you want from a man?"

*A future.*

"Savannah, dear," Olive began in a motherly tone,

"what's the real problem? I'm looking in your eyes and all I see is pain. If it's because of his trysts with Ruthie from the café, I can assure you that was never serious and it ended years ago."

"It does bother me," she admitted. "What if the same happens with me? We could end the same way if we...did anything about the situation."

"Pooh! If anyone was using anyone in that situation, it was Ruthie using Seth. She just wants a father for that incorrigible child of hers and Seth is good with the boy. Though only the good Lord knows why. If you ask me, he's a lost cause."

Savannah smiled. "Seth had him picking up trash at the wildlife preserve yesterday."

That gave Olive a good belly laugh. "I would have paid to see that. It's probably good experience for the kid."

"I thought so."

"No," Olive corrected. "I meant it was good experience for his future. He'll probably be part of a prison crew cleaning up the highways and scenic roads before too long."

Savannah felt herself frown. So she didn't really know the boy, that was true. But she had seen some things in him the day before that gave her reason to think there might be hope for Cal. She guessed his bad behavior was that of a typical teenager crying for attention.

"He listened to Seth," Savannah finally said.

"Always has," Olive said. "Seth is the closest thing that boy has had to a father. I've always believed that Seth maintained his *friendship* with Ruthie just so he could keep tabs on the kid." Olive sighed. "I guess I was lucky. Junior has never given me a moment of trouble."

Savannah could believe that. Junior was just too sweet and devoted to his ailing mother to be anything but the ideal son.

"Speaking of Junior, where is he this morning?"

Olive seemed to be fighting back a frown. She was always unhappy when her pride and joy wasn't around. "It's tax season," she explained. "He had to meet with three or four clients today. It was my idea for him to become an accountant, you know."

Savannah began to straighten a basket of seeds. "No. Why an accountant?"

Olive's expression grew hard for a second. It was strange, since she'd never seen the woman express anything other than happiness, or pain and sorrow over the loss of her husband decades earlier.

"I wanted him to do good, stable work. I think a man should be financially secure, don't you?"

"Sure," Savannah agreed easily. "Especially when he gets married and has a family."

"My Junior won't ever marry," Olive said with complete conviction.

Savannah stopped her task and asked, "Why would you think that?"

"I don't *think* it," Olive answered. "I know it. Junior knows I need him. Some days I can barely get around with my arthritis. Besides, we've been close ever since my husband died. I don't think we could ever live apart. I also explained to him that no woman would be interested in him, being a package deal and all."

Savannah could have argued those points in several ways. Instead she chose to hold her tongue. If the arrangement worked for them then who was she to challenge it? Besides, Junior was totally devoted to his mother. He had a career he seemed to enjoy. And for all she knew, maybe he truly wasn't interested in a having a family of his own. Olive was right on one account. None of the women she had ever known would have embraced the idea of marrying a man who came with apron strings tied in a double knot.

"What about you?" Olive asked. "Do you want to marry and have a family?"

She nodded, nearly choking up at the question.

"Then why don't you do both with Seth?"

"Olive," Savannah warned. "Can we please talk about something other than Seth?"

The bell tinkled as the door opened and Seth came inside the shop. He was immediately aware of some tension in the room and he noted pink tints on Savannah's cheeks.

"Should my ears be burning?" he asked.

"Absolutely," Olive replied with a wicked grin. "I've spent the better part of the morning trying to convince her to marry you and have babies."

"Olive!" Savannah uttered the two syllables through a clenched jaw.

"Shouldn't you check with me first?" Seth asked teasingly.

Olive snorted. "I don't need to ask you. I've known you since you were in diapers, Seth Landry. I can tell you're smitten with my Savannah."

"Guilty."

Savannah's blush worsened.

"So how come you aren't doing anything about it?"

"Who says I'm not? The problem is your hard-headed employee."

"Can we please change the subject?" Savannah pleaded. "Besides, my shift is over, so we really don't have the time to dissect my personal life. Which, if anyone cares, I'd prefer to keep private."

"In Jasper?" Olive huffed. "The whole town already thinks you two are an item. Jake from the gas station saw Seth's Bronco parked at your house all night. Half a dozen people have reported that the two of you are inseparable. You might as well just go for it."

Seth met and held Savannah's gaze. "Good advice, Olive."

"Bad advice," Savannah countered as she got her

purse and coat from behind the counter. "I'm leaving, but the two of you are welcome to stay and chat."

Seth smothered his grin and said, "No, I'm taking you to lunch."

"A date?" Olive asked optimistically.

"Sure," Seth said.

"No," Savannah countered at almost the same time.

They left with the sound of Olive's laughter chasing them.

Savannah waited until they got into the Bronco before she gave him a glare that was virtually deadly.

"What?"

"You had no right to tell Olive those things. Now she'll think there really is something between us and she won't let up on me."

Seth no longer bothered to contain his smile. "That was the whole point."

Seth backed out of the parking spot and turned south. Which was pretty much where Savannah's mood was at the moment. He had a feeling it wasn't going to get any better when she fully realized just where he was taking her for lunch.

A few minutes later, her outburst of, "I'm not going in *there* with *you*," proved his suspicion.

"The Cowboy Café serves great food, and since your idea of breakfast is a pot of coffee, you need to eat."

Clearly sulking, she said, "I'm not hungry."

"Well, I am," he countered. "We might have one awkward moment, but I promise you the food will be worth it."

"How could meeting your mistress be worth anything to me?"

"Former girlfriend," he corrected. "I had a productive morning. I just assumed you'd like a full update."

Her mood lightened. "I would. But why does it have to be here?"

Seth reached out and caught her chin between his thumb and forefinger. "It has to be here because I don't feel right avoiding Ruthie because I'm with you. I've told you. We are friends."

"What about how Ruthie feels?"

He shrugged. "So long as I promise her I'll still help her out with Cal, she's happy. Trust me, I've been honest with her. She knew this would come someday, and I promised her we'd always be friends. I plan on honoring that."

"She may plan on dumping a plate of food in your lap."

"Please cooperate?" Seth fairly purred.

When he spoke to her in that tone *and* touched her, it was virtually impossible for her to refuse him anything. "Okay, but if she starts a scene, I'm outta there."

Seth treated her to one of his heart-stopping smiles. "Thank you."

Though she'd been to the café about a half a dozen times, Savannah now approached the door with great trepidation. Seth reached around her and grasped the handle. A rush of hot air hit her as she preceded him into the restaurant.

As was normal, the place was virtually filled. There was only one booth available, so she and Seth walked the entire length of the narrow, diner-shaped room.

The abnormal part was the looks she was getting from the patrons and the servers. She felt about as welcome as a cockroach and was regretting the fact that she had let Seth talk her into this.

The buzz of conversation lowered to mere whispers as they took their seats. Intentionally, Savannah slipped into the bench that allowed her to keep her back to everyone. Seth reached out and touched her fingertips with his. She knew it was supposed to be a gesture of comfort, but the butterflies in her stomach didn't seem to notice.

"Hey, darling."

Hearing Ruthie's familiar greeting to Seth didn't sit well. She experienced a bout of jealousy more severe than she had ever known. Intellectually, she understood the relationship between the two and she believed Seth when he said it was over. Emotionally, she felt the odd urge to stick out her tongue and say, "He's mine now."

Instead, she simply said "Thank you" when

Ruthie handed her a well-worn menu. For a brief instant, their eyes met. Amazingly, Ruthie didn't look the least bit upset. For the life of her Savannah couldn't grasp that. If she'd just lost Seth to another woman, she'd be glaring fireballs at her replacement.

*What am I thinking? He isn't mine to lose!*

"Thanks for getting that gun away from Cal," Ruthie said to Seth. "I hate to think of the trouble he'd find with something so dangerous."

"It was no problem," Seth assured her. His tone was easy, as if he were chatting with a friend instead of a former lover.

Was it possible that he had been right? That Ruthie wasn't fazed by the demise of their relationship?

"You're Savannah from Olive's, right?" Ruthie inquired pleasantly.

"Yes."

"It's good to meet you."

Lord, this woman was either a great actress or the most understanding woman on the face of the earth. She decided to take Ruthie at face value.

"You, too," Savannah returned with a genuine smile. "I've been in a few times before, but just for carryout."

"Well, hopefully Seth can change that," Ruthie said on a laugh. "I swear I don't think the man knows how to cook. If he did, he wouldn't eat here at every chance."

"I'm afraid I'm no help in that department. I use my oven for storage," Savannah joked back.

Ruthie made a tsking sound. "Well, if you decide you want some lessons, give me a call."

"I might just do that," Savannah said. "Eating microwaved meals does get a little old after a while."

"Do you need some time to look at the menu, or do you know what you want?"

Savannah explained that she would need a few minutes, so Ruthie agreed to return after a bit. She also noticed that Seth hadn't even bothered to open his menu. And she noticed that he was wearing his killer smile.

"What?"

"I'm impressed."

"Why?"

"I thought that went rather well. Now do you believe that I didn't break her heart?"

Savannah nodded. "Yes. She seems like a very nice woman. I'm not sure I could be that civil to a woman who replaced me in your—"

"My what?" Seth pressed, his grin widening.

Savannah pretended to scan the menu until she thought of an appropriate cover story. "I was speaking theoretically. *If* you and I were involved, I'm not sure I could handle it as well as Ruthie appears to be."

Seth captured one of her hands in both of his. There was a hint of amusement in his ebony eyes. "Savannah, like it or not, we *are* involved."

Letting out a long sigh, Savannah felt the familiar sensation of her heart being torn in two. "We're not. Because you would never leave Jasper."

He began to make small, sensual circles against her palm.

"Maybe I would. If it meant we could stay together."

She was shaking her head violently when Ruthie returned to take their orders. Savannah settled on a turkey burger and bottled water while Seth went all out and ordered a portion of steak that she could have made three meals from.

If Ruthie noticed the intimate gesture he was making on her hand, she showed no outward signs. In fact, she was still maintaining her cheerful attitude.

"I would *never* ask you to leave Jasper," Savannah said as soon as they were alone. "You wouldn't just be leaving behind your career, you'd be cut off from your family. You couldn't be godfather to Callie and Sam's baby and you couldn't punch Shane whenever he annoyed you. Are you honestly telling me that you'd give all that up for me?"

Seth leaned forward and in a hushed tone said, "I might have to. I love you, Savannah."

She closed her eyes for a minute. "*Maybe* you lust for me," she countered. "Lord knows we have a combustible sexual chemistry, but you haven't known me long enough to love me."

"Says who?" he challenged defensively.

"Logic. It wouldn't be fair to you or your family if you made some rash decision and disappeared from their lives. Believe me, I know."

"Believe me," Seth returned with annoyance. "I love you and I think you feel the same way about me."

"I *can't* feel that way."

It was his turn to sigh. "Keep telling yourself that lie, Savannah. But I promise you, it won't hold up for long. Luckily I'm a patient man. I can wait to hear you say the words."

Thankfully, their food arrived, which put an abrupt end to the uncomfortable conversation. *Uncomfortable?* she asked her brain, *or just truthful?* No! He couldn't be right. It was just lust, she insisted to the annoying voice inside her head. She wanted him, which was the problem. Maybe if she just did it and got it out of her system, she could return to normal.

"Are you going to eat?" Seth asked.

Savannah immediately picked up her burger and took a small bite. It was good, except for the undertaste of bacon from the air. That couldn't be helped. No matter the time of day, the café always smelled of bacon and coffee.

"So what good things did you find out today?" she asked as she put the burger back on her plate. Somehow Seth's proclamation of love had dampened her appetite for food. However, it had increased her appetite for another form of sustenance. Placing her hand beneath the table, she jabbed her fingernails into her palm in an attempt to shut off her hormones. It seemed to be a continual problem when she was around Seth. One she either had to control or act upon.

"I found out how the Saint Barnabas medal ended up in my bedroom."

"How?"

"Someone jimmied the lock on my basement door."

"That's scary," Savannah said. "Do you think Updyke, Angelica or Lurch would have the nerve to break into the town sheriff's house?"

"It was probably Updyke. The ballistics on Angelica's .22 proved it wasn't the murder weapon."

"I still don't understand why the killer left the medal at your house. According to Olive, everyone and their brother knows you're sleeping at my house. Why not put it there?"

Seth's brows drew together. "Probably to make a point. Taunt me a little. The killer knows I'm investigating, so my guess is he was just toying with me."

"I think he wanted to freak you out so you'd back off on the investigation," Savannah offered. "He probably thinks that if he can get you out of the picture, he'll have a clear shot at me."

"I'm staying in the picture," Seth said with conviction. "As we dine, I'm having an alarm system put in my house and I called Shane and he's sending over some of the hands to stand guard at night."

She smiled. "I guess it's convenient to have ranch hands at your disposal."

"It is," he agreed easily. "We've used them before. Every one of them is a decent shot."

"But not as decent as you, right?" She grinned when her compliment stained his cheeks pink for an instant.

"I also had Mable run a check on registered .22s in Lewis and Clark County."

"Wouldn't Updyke have brought his own gun?"

Seth nodded. "Yes. But I thought as a precaution I'd like knowing who has a .22 in the area."

"Who does?"

His expression deflated. "Unfortunately, more than three hundred of our friends and neighbors."

"That many?" Savannah asked, astonished.

"Yep, and that list includes Mable, Angelica, Olive and almost every other person in town. Even Sam bought one for Callie a few months back."

"I've never seen a gun in Olive's shop," Savannah said.

"I'm sure you haven't. It was registered twenty-six years ago by her husband."

"It gets worse," he admitted. "There are more than a thousand registered .22s in the Gold West Country. I wish I had the manpower to check every last one of them, but I don't."

"Well, you've already ruled out Angelica. I'm sure we can rule out Callie and Olive, as well. I'm sure your sister-in-law isn't a pregnant hitwoman and Olive's hands are so gnarled from arthritis I doubt she could pull a trigger." She pushed her plate away.

"You didn't eat much," Seth observed.

"I ate enough," she promised him. *I ate as much as I could considering the fact that you told me you loved me.*

Seth paid the check and he and Ruthie shared a very pleasant goodbye. The waitress even insisted he bring Savannah back on meat loaf night.

Seth took her to her house so they could both pack to stay at his newly alarmed home. Savannah packed lightly then threw in a heavy ankle-length skirt at the last minute, just in case she needed to dress for something.

Seth carried his duffel and her small bag and headed out the door ahead of her to load the Bronco. Savannah was in the process of locking the door when she heard it.

Spinning around, she turned just in time to see Seth get hit in the head by the bullet.

## Chapter Thirteen

Mindless of his injury, Seth lunged at Savannah, covering her body with his own. He stayed that way for several minutes, until he was as sure as he could be that no more shots were to be fired. Making sure to shield her, Seth urged her to crawl in front of him across the front porch to the door where the keys still hung in the lock.

After opening the door, he said, "Stay on your belly. When we get inside, stay away from the windows."

"Don't worry, I will," Savannah answered, her voice tremulous. "You're bleeding."

"I'll live," Seth said, annoyed that he'd almost

failed to protect her. Visions of Savannah lying dead on the porch haunted him as he worked his way inside, then over to the phone.

His first call was to his deputies. "I want every available unit to Savannah's cabin right now. Call the state police for reinforcements," he instructed as he felt Savannah press a soft cloth against the left side of his head. It barely stung, which he knew meant he'd only been grazed. "I want them to search every inch within a half mile of the cabin." He then went on to explain what had happened.

His second call was to Chance.

"You got shot?" his brother asked with genuine concern.

"I don't think it's serious," Seth said.

"Can you get out of there safely?" Chance asked.

"I've called for backup. I doubt the shooter is going to stick around when this place is swarming with cops."

"You're closer to the Lucky 7 than town. I'll head out now and meet you there. Are you sure you don't need to go to the hospital?" Chance queried.

"I'm sure. At best I'll need a stitch or two."

Savannah piped up with, "I don't know, Seth. It's bleeding profusely."

"Head wounds always bleed," he told her.

Chance interjected, "Let me be the one to make the diagnosis. Is Savannah hurt?"

Seth glanced in her direction and with the exception of a bruise on her cheek—most probably from his tackling her on the hard wooden porch—she appeared shaken but fine.

"You might want to look her over. She's pretty shaken. See you at the ranch." He hung up and took the towel from Savannah and applied more pressure with his own hand.

"I don't need a doctor," Savannah argued.

Distant sirens grew closer, then they heard several cars come to a screeching halt just outside the door.

"Stay down," Seth said as he worked his way back to the door and slowly opened it.

J.D. had followed his instructions to a tee. There were cars from the county, the state and two neighboring towns outside. The state SWAT van was also waiting.

Wearing protective black suits, vests and carrying shields, two of the SWAT guys made their way to the door.

"Sheriff Landry?" the older of the two inquired.

"Yes."

The two men introduced themselves, then asked, "How bad is your head wound?"

"Not bad," he assured them. "I was standing in front of the Bronco when I was hit. I think he was aiming for Savannah. She was here," he indicated Savannah's position, "so, my guess is the shooter was someplace up there near those boulders."

"Savannah?"

"She's fine," Seth told the specialized officer.

"We'll get you an ambulance."

"Not necessary," Seth replied. "I just need cover to get out of here. I'm meeting my brother at our ranch. He'll fix me up."

"Your call," the officer said, obviously not in agreement with the plan. "But I don't think you should be driving with a head wound."

"I won't. Savannah can drive. Just get me two cars to flank the Bronco until we're on the highway."

"Done."

"And I want every inch of this property searched. I think we're looking for a guy named Updyke." Seth gave a description of the amateur hitman. "Hopefully he left some forensics behind this time."

Seth went back inside and explained to Savannah what they were going to do.

"Is it safe?" she asked. "Shouldn't I drive you to the hospital? Your head is still bleeding."

He gave her his brightest smile. "You can give me another towel to ruin. You can buy yourself new ones with the hundred bucks I owe you from our bet."

She responded with a burst of anger. "I don't give a damn about towels or silly bets. I care about you getting proper medical treatment. I can't stand knowing you got hurt because of me."

Seth winked at her. "See, you do care."

"Don't start with me, Landry," she warned. "Getting shot at doesn't bring out the best in me."

Their pseudoargument was interrupted by the SWAT members who had come to take them to the Bronco. Seth flipped her the keys. "I think I'll let you drive this time."

"Thanks."

It didn't take the trained SWAT team long to get them and their bags into the Bronco. It was a bit of a tight squeeze for Seth, since there were matching SUVs on either side of his.

"I can't reach the pedals," Savannah said.

Seth explained the console on the armrest and she soon had the seat and mirrors in a position to start the engine. The minute she did, two others followed.

Only they turned on their sirens, which didn't do much for the headache Seth had coming on at a record pace. Luckily, the two official vehicles left off when they were safely on the highway, headed for home.

Seth winced inwardly at that thought. Could he really do what Savannah suggested? Could he leave his career, his home, his family and heritage to join her in the Witness Protection Program? It was a tough call. So was imagining his life without her in it.

She'd been right about one thing. He didn't think he could handle abandonment again. Even after a decade, he still felt the loss of his parents deeply. And he felt anger. How could they have done that?

"Are you conscious?" Savannah asked.

"No," he teased, hoping to ease some of the tension he heard in her voice.

"How's the bleeding?" she asked.

"Bloody."

"Has anyone ever told you you're a real smart-ass when you've been shot?"

"Never been shot before," Seth replied. "The gate is about a half mile up."

"I remember," Savannah said. "I'll feel a lot better once Chance has seen to your wound."

Seth slipped his free hand over and rested it on her leg. "Thank you for that."

"That what?"

"Your unintentional admission that you care what happens to me. It has revived my hope."

"I do care," she said.

He watched her grip tighten on the wheel.

"You know I do," she continued. "But there are just too many obstacles in our way for us to start anything."

"What if we didn't have those obstacles?" he asked just as she parked in front of the house.

Savannah never had an opportunity to answer. Virtually the whole house came bounding down the stairs to open the door and help him inside.

Sam and Shane insisted on holding his arms as they climbed the steps. Taylor was waiting at the top with a fresh towel. Callie looked horrified, but apparently it was her assigned task to look after Savannah.

His brothers helped him up to his room. It had an adjoining bathroom, so Chance would have everything at his disposal. When he got around to showing up.

"IT'S ALL MY FAULT," Savannah was telling Sam, Shane and Callie. She couldn't help but wonder what Chance was doing upstairs. It seemed as if an eternity had passed since he had climbed the steps with his bag.

"You can't blame yourself," Sam told her. "You aren't responsible for the actions of a deranged person, is she Callie?"

Callie shook her head. "I had something similar happen to me almost a year ago. Just be grateful that you and Seth are alive, well and together."

"They aren't together," Taylor added candidly. "Though only the Lord himself knows why."

Savannah was being stared at by four sets of surprised eyes. "What?" she almost snapped.

Sam cleared his throat and said, "I was under the impression that you and my brother shared…a mutual interest."

She chuckled at his attempt to be delicate. "We share a common physical attraction," she said. "There is no future in a relationship based solely on chemistry."

Callie went over and sat on her husband's lap. In spite of her pregnancy-swollen body, Sam seemed thrilled to have her so close. His hands went to her belly, feeling for signs of the life they had created together.

"Where's your older son?" Savannah asked.

"We didn't know how badly Seth was injured, so we had one of the hands take him to a friend's house."

"Smart," Savannah said.

"No," Callie began politely but firmly. "Smart is recognizing when you've found your soul mate and not letting him slip away. I almost made that mistake with Sam, and I'd hate to see it happen with you and Seth."

"Nothing has happened with her and Seth," Taylor supplied as she refilled everyone's coffee cups.

"May I ask why?" Callie asked with gentleness. "I'm sure you don't need me to tell you what a wonderful man Seth is."

Hugging the steaming mug of coffee, Savannah tried to think of an answer that had a touch of truth. "I move around a lot. I can't stay in one place for long and Seth is very rooted here in Jasper."

"That's true," Sam admitted. "Are you sure you couldn't give putting down roots a try?"

"I'm sure," she answered honestly.

The telephone interrupted the inquisition. Sam answered, then surprisingly passed the phone to Savannah.

"Hello?"

"It's Cody," he said, sounding majorly pissed. "How is my brother?"

"Chance is still with him."

"Then go find out. I'll talk to Sam while you're gone. Then I have some news for you."

As Savannah passed the phone back to Sam, she was on the verge of tears. She knew that because of the shooting, especially since it was his own brother, Cody was going to relocate her yet again.

She climbed the stairs and listened for Chance's voice. Following the sound, she found the two of them in the next to last room on the left.

Chance was putting stitches in Seth's head and Seth was providing unkind critique as he went along.

Savannah lightly knocked on the open door.

"Come in and see what a terrible seamstress my brother is," Seth invited jovially. Then he must have seen the hurt and anguish in her eyes because he said, "What's wrong?"

"C-Cody is on the phone," she managed to choke out as she battled tears. "He wants to know how you are and then he'll give me some more information I'll tell you about." She turned to leave.

"Wait!' Seth commanded. "How much longer are you going to be?" he barked at his brother.

"Last stitch."

"Good, then can you give us some privacy."

Chance looked from Savannah to Seth and made haste.

He closed his door on the way out, saying he would write out instructions for him to follow.

The minute they were alone, Savannah burst into tears. She was in Seth's arms in an instant with him placing light kisses on the top of her head. "He's going to relocate me again," she said.

"He said that?"

"No, but he told me to get back on the phone with him after I found out how you were. He was pretty mad at me for getting you shot."

"Obviously my brother doesn't always think straight." Seth moved away from her and went to an extension on the nightstand. "Sam, hang up. I need to talk to Cody now."

Savannah brushed away the remnants of her tears. She couldn't remember the last time she had cried. Lately it seemed as if it was the only thing she wanted to do.

"Really?" Seth said into the receiver. "That's great news on both counts." There was a long pause before Seth said, "And Cody, if you ever make Savannah cry again, they won't be able to identify you with dental records."

After he hung up, he went to the door, opened it and yelled for Chance.

"What was good news?" she asked.

"I'll tell you as soon as Chance checks you out."

"I'm fine," she insisted as the doctor reentered the room.

"She's an emotional wreck," Seth told Chance.

"I am not," Savannah insisted.

"Let's see." Chance opened his bag and got out a blood pressure cuff and a stethoscope. He checked her pulse, her heart rate and her blood pressure. "You're pretty stressed," he concurred.

"So I'll take some deep breaths," Savannah promised.

"If that doesn't work," he said as he reached into his bag, "take one of these before bedtime." He turned to Seth and added, "As for you, I want someone to wake you up every forty-five minutes during the night to make sure you're coherent. Without an X ray, I don't know if the graze wound was enough to cause a concussion."

Savannah stuffed the pill into her pocket and volunteered. "I'll stay up with him."

Chance looked at her and said, "He needs rest."

Savannah rolled her eyes. "Does every member of this family think we're lovers?"

Chance seemed taken aback. "Well, I thought—"

"Wrong," Seth said in her defense.

Shrugging, Chance pulled a card from his wallet and said, "Okay then. Here's my home and pager numbers. Call me if he stops making sense or develops any additional symptoms like blurred vision."

"I will."

*Landry's Law*

"I'll be by tomorrow at lunchtime to check on you," Chance said to his brother. I want you to stay glued to that bed until I say so."

Seth's response was both vivid and vulgar.

"You, too," Chance said before he left the room.

"What did Cody say?" Savannah asked on a rush of breath.

"Come and lie with me," Seth asked.

"Seth!"

"Just lie," he said, making a cross sign over his heart. "I'm more comfortable lying down."

Savannah complied, going to the far side of the king-size bed and stretching out. Apparently that wasn't good enough for Seth. He refused to tell her anything about his conversation with Cody until she was nestled in his arms.

"He has a lead on Updyke. They expect to pick him up tomorrow or the next day."

"Here in Jasper?"

"No, New York."

"Then who shot you today?"

"That's the sixty-four thousand dollar question," Seth agreed. "There's more good news."

"What?" Savannah asked. She felt her stress draining away just from being in his arms. Tucked safely away at the ranch in Seth's arms seemed like the place she was meant to be. Suddenly, Connecticut sounded like a place to visit, not live.

"Rossi is dying of cancer."

"Calling that good news is a little bit cold, even if he is a crime boss."

"Well, he's a crime boss who apparently no longer cares about the trial."

Savannah sat bolt upright. "He doesn't want me dead?"

"Not him personally," Seth said. "He ordered that the contract on your life be canceled."

"Then I'm home free?"

Seth pulled her back into his embrace. "We won't know that until they arrest Updyke. He was sent here by someone. It could be that some underboss also facing charges has reinstated the contract."

"Great," Savannah mumbled against his chest. "So obviously Updyke left town and they've sent someone new."

"If they have, we'll find him," Seth promised as he kissed her head. "If and until that happens, I'll keep you safe, Savannah."

"What about you?" she said as the room fell into total darkness after the sunset.

"I'm tough."

"You got hurt because of me."

"Thank God," he said.

"How can you say that?" Savannah gasped.

"Because the alternative would have been that the bullet hit you. I love you too much to watch you die."

*Me, too.* "You'd better get some rest."

"Keep lying to yourself, Savannah. I can wait to hear you say it."

SETH HAD PASSED every test during the night and was up and brushing his teeth just after Savannah had vacated the bathroom.

He finished and gave her an odd look.

"What?"

"You don't usually wear skirts," he commented as he came out of the bathroom wearing his jeans and a shirt. The top button of his jeans wasn't done up, nor were the top three of his shirt. The shower had washed all the traces of blood from his hair and he looked perfectly normal. Correction—he looked perfect.

"How's your head?"

He brushed his hand over the small bandage and said, "I don't notice it at all. But I do have some wonderful recollections of you waking me during the night. I almost feigned disorientation just to see if I could get you to admit that you love me."

"It isn't going to happen," she warned again. "Even your family agrees that you'd be miserable anywhere but Jasper, and I can't stay here."

Seth reached her in two long strides. "So, your goal is still to work your way back to Connecticut. You know, pick up your old life and all that?"

She lowered her eyes. "My old life doesn't exist anymore. And to tell you the truth, I do like it here."

His expression darkened as his eyes made a bold appraisal of her. "Since we're discussing truthfulness, I feel it only appropriate that I tell you that you have lied to me in the past."

"Really?"

He closed the distance between them in a few long strides. "You lied when you refused to kiss me good-night. So to make it up to me, I can think of nothing that would give me more pleasure than to kiss you now," he said, bending down.

He kissed her with a hard, hungry pressure that thrilled her. Her hands lifted quickly to his shirt, tearing open the edges in order to feel the rough silkiness of the dark hair covering his chest. She pushed the garment down his arms, feeling the power in his bunched muscles.

"I think I like your aggressive tendencies," he teased as he allowed what was left of his shirt to fall to the floor. "But I guess two can play your game."

That said, Seth grasped the top of her blouse and tore the first few buttons before regaining control. The noise she made against his mouth wasn't one of protest, it was sheer pleasure knowing that he wanted her as desperately as she wanted him. Blouses were replaceable. This sort of passion came along only once in a lifetime.

His mouth slowed to a gentler pace as his hand

cupped the swell of her breast. Savannah moaned and pressed herself against him, caught between wanting this to last all day and the overwhelming urgency coiling her stomach.

His expression was kind and gentle and Savannah silently acknowledged that she would have been lost without him. *I love you, Seth* she thought, but didn't dare say. He kissed her then set her down gently.

Savannah looked at the half-open door. "We should be discreet. I don't want to have to explain us having an affair to anyone."

"Who said we were having an affair?" he asked as he went to lock the door.

"The whole town."

He moved to stand in front of her. Savannah stood, closing the small space between them. Reaching up, she gently ran the tip of her fingernail near the bottom of his lower lip. She could feel the outline of his powerfully built thighs where they rubbed hers.

His expression stilled and grew serious when Savannah pressed herself against him. Seth placed his hands at her waist. For an instant she thought he might push her away.

"I'm very sure about this, so don't push me away," she beseeched. "Please? I can't run from you any-more."

His hesitation lasted less than a second before his lips found hers. Tentative and testing, his mouth settled over hers. She responded by allowing her lips to part, urging his sweet exploration. He groaned as his arms encircled her, pulling her so close that Savannah could feel every solid inch of him.

Her mind reeled from the blatant sensuality of his kiss. It was as if a flash fire had ignited and it was quickly burning out of control. Her hands moved down from his face until she could feel his heart beat furiously. He gripped her more tightly, causing her back to arch. Seth moaned against her mouth.

Emotions and sensations melted together and coursed through her veins. Every cell in her body tingled with life. Guided by the powerful force of her desire, Savannah ran her palms over his warm flesh. His breath fell hotly over her skin when he lifted his head. She was about to utter a protest when he lifted her off the ground and carried her toward the bed.

Seth pressed his lips to her throat, tasting the faintly floral scent of her skin. She felt so delicate, and yet the strength of her passion completely amazed him. This was going to change things between them forever. He didn't want to think about it now. If he did, he knew he'd have to stop. *Not this time.*

He put her on the bed and lay beside her, his one leg wedged between hers. Placing his hand at her waist, Seth kissed the tip of her nose before renewing his interest in her throat. He felt her intake of breath when his fingers inched upward then closed over the top of one rounded breast. He could feel the taut nipple pressing against his palm and that knowledge sent waves of urgent desire to his loins. Each caress seemed to make her want more and he was more than willing to give it.

Slowly, deliberately, he toyed with each button, kissing the areas that became exposed to his hungry eyes. Her skin was smooth, rich and pale under his hand. Seth was finding it hard to exercise discipline. Lifting his head, he looked at her flushed face briefly before turning his attention lower. Her fingers fanned out across his chest as he loomed above her, eyes fixed on her lacy black bra. His finger dipped inside, teasing the hard nipple. It wasn't enough.

Undoing the clasp, Seth peeled away the barrier. She made a small sound when his mouth closed around the tip of her breast. He felt her hands on his neck, holding him against her as she arched upward, toward him. Each time he flicked the tip of her nipple with his tongue, Savannah moaned and pressed her hips against his leg.

Pulling at her skirt, Seth reached beneath it and placed his hand on her thigh. His fingertips barely brushed the sensitive inside but he could already feel her responding. Her hands moved across his shoulders, massaging and molding.

Heat merged with pressure in his groin when she made brief, shy contact with his partially opened waistband. She explored the contours of his sex through his jeans. He found the silky edge of her panties and worked his fingers inside.

He almost lost all control then, spurred by his incredible passion for this woman. He lifted his head and kissed her fiercely. His hand lingered at the waistband of her panties as he lay beside her on the bed. He teased her through the flimsy fabric for a moment, reveling in the response it inspired. Savannah thrust her body toward him, all the while matching his demanding kiss. He could smell the faint scent of her perfume.

Seth lifted his head again, watching the stain of redness on her flushed face.

"You're embarrassing me."

He liked the husky, sexy tone of her voice and simply smiled down at her. "I don't think you have a thing to be embarrassed about."

"Why are you staring at me?"

"I'm not staring, sweetheart. I'm admiring," he said just before lowering his mouth to capture one rosy nipple in his mouth. She responded instantly. Savannah's fingers carefully played through the hair on the uninjured side of his head as he lovingly taunted each rounded peak in turn. Every now and again he would hear a moan from her and respond by placing a kiss on her partly opened mouth.

When he could no longer stand the pressure at his groin, Seth began to remove her skirt, then his own clothing. He pushed her back against the pillow, using his knee to wedge himself between her legs. He remained balanced above her, watching the expression on her face when his hips met hers. There was still the barrier of their underclothes and he needed her reassurance.

"I want to make love to you, Savannah."

"I want that, too. Very much."

He moved only long enough to remove the last hindrance of their clothing. He could tell almost immediately that she was as ready as he was. Seth had to school himself to move slowly. She wasn't helping him at all as she continued to grind her slender body against his.

"Slow down, Savannah, or this won't last more than about ten seconds."

His mouth covered hers before she could speak, though he had a hunch she was beyond the point of lucid conversation. Carefully he entered her, listening for—even expecting—some sort of protest or hesitation. Instead he heard only words of pleasure whispered on a warm breath against his mouth.

With a single thrust, he gloried in being deep inside such sweet softness. When she wound her legs around him, Seth groaned and fervently kissed her neck and shoulders before returning to the warm, pliant recesses of her mouth. The rhythm of their lovemaking increased as his hands reached beneath her hips, bringing her even closer to him.

She turned her face away from his, breaking their kiss. "Something wonderful is happening to me," she told him, her eyes wide, her pupils dilated with passion.

"Go with it, sweetheart."

As predicted, he felt her body convulse with wave after pleasurable wave. The sensation of having her body grip him brought Seth to a fast and furious release.

Savannah could have stayed there forever. Apparently afraid of crushing her with his weight, Seth rolled off her, leaving Savannah to wonder at the incredible things her body had just experienced. She was also a bit surprised by the fact that she was no longer concerned about her nakedness. Turning her head, she smiled at her lover.

He returned the gesture.

"That was incredible," she told him. Savannah turned in his arms and placed a kiss on his chest. Her fingers toyed with his chest hair as she listened as his breath returned to normal. They stayed that way for a while.

"I don't want to go to work," she muttered as she glanced over at the clock.

Seth kissed her forehead. "When do you have to leave?"

"I've got about fifteen minutes before I have to shower again and redress."

"I wish we had more time," he said.

Hearing the yearning in his voice, Savannah was secretly pleased by his pleasure in their lovemaking. "We'll have time later today."

Then his pager started beeping.

## Chapter Fourteen

Savannah took a quick shower, dressed in her jeans since her skirt was all crumpled on Seth's floor, and managed to apply some makeup. All this in under fifteen minutes.

When she emerged from the bathroom, Seth was still on the bed speaking to his office and Taylor was standing in the doorway.

Taylor's eyes apparently didn't miss Seth's mussed hair or the fact that he was still naked, with just the sheet pulled over his lap.

She gave Savannah a knowing grin before saying, "Junior Baumgartner is downstairs."

"Junior?" she repeated.

"He said his mother sent him to drive you to work. I guess news of the shooting is already common knowledge in Jasper."

"Great," Savannah breathed. She went over and kissed Seth's cheek as she swung her purse on her arm. "I'll see you later," she told him.

Seth instantly covered the phone and said, "Where do you think you're going?"

"To work," she reminded him.

"Not until I finish my call. Then I'll drive you in."

"No need," she insisted. "Olive must have heard all about the shooting so she sent Junior out here to drive me in. I guess they think you're too wounded to drive me to work."

Seth's brow furrowed. "I'd rather you waited."

Savannah blew out a breath and raked her hair off her face. "This is Junior we're talking about," she reminded him. "You've known him since grade school."

"I'm not worried about Junior, I'm worried about our shooter." He sighed, then said, "Go ahead, I'll have J.D. or Greg meet you at the shop until I can get there."

"You're supposed to stay in bed until Chance comes to check on you," she said, wagging her finger near his face. "Try to be a good patient."

"Something like that," he said, then he returned to his call.

She found Junior in the foyer, having a polite

conversation with Callie. He turned when she reached the bottom step. His smile was warm and reached his magnified eyes. Having glasses that made your eyes the size of wafers wasn't very attractive. But then neither was Junior.

He was short, slightly pudgy and balding. It was a shame he didn't have more self-confidence, because she knew him to be a truly nice man.

"Hi," she greeted warmly.

"Hi, yourself," he returned easily. "Mother and I were so upset when we heard what happened. You got bruised," he said, his face filled with concern.

Vainly, Savannah placed her hand over her cheek and said, "This is nothing. Seth was the one who got hurt."

"How badly?" Junior asked.

Savannah smiled broadly. "Luckily it was just a graze-type wound. It only took two stitches to close it."

Callie was also smiling. "I guess he must have been restless. Every time I walked past his room this morning I could hear movement inside."

Savannah felt her face grow hot. "Well, if I'm going to get to work on time, we should probably go."

"Okay," Junior agreed.

"It really was sweet of you to come all the way out here," Savannah repeated as they left the house.

"I didn't mind."

"It's a long drive from town," Savannah said as he held the door to his sedan open for her.

She noticed that there were grocery sacks in the back and a cooler. Maybe Junior had stopped at the warehouse food place on his way out to the Lucky 7. Lord knew Olive loved to cook and Junior loved to eat.

"Ready?" he asked when he had the key in the lock.

"I've got my purse and my coat. I travel light," she teased.

"Then I guess it's time for us to be off."

Junior drove the quarter mile down the driveway to the highway. But he didn't turn right toward Jasper.

"Do you have an errand to run?" she asked.

"Kind of," Junior hesitated. He reached into the pocket of his overcoat and pulled out a small black gun.

"What are you doing?" she asked, stunned at the unexpected turn of events.

"I'm taking you to my special place," he said.

"Why?"

"So that we can be alone."

"Alone for what?"

Laying the gun in his lap for a moment, he reached over and placed his stumpy fingers over her knee. "Alone so that we can be together."

Savannah was scared, angry and planning all at once. "We can be together at the shop," she tried to reason as he turned up a logging road that she hadn't even noticed during her ride with Seth.

"I tried to keep you pure for me," Junior said. "It almost worked."

"Pure?"

"I couldn't let you sleep with those men my mother set you up with. Not when I've loved you since the first day we met."

*Junior was the killer. And she was trapped!*

CODY WAS WAITING for him at his office when Seth came in around eleven. He was smiling like the proverbial cat who ate the canary.

"What?" Seth asked as he went to the window to check that Greg was parked outside of Olive's. He was, so Seth gave his brother his full attention.

"Guess who just got taken off the Rossi case," Cody fairly crowed.

"You?"

"Peter White."

"The Justice Department guy whose been dragging his heels for six years?"

"None other. Care to know how the J.D. found out about his alleged financial dealings with the Rossi family?"

"Yes."

"They arrested Updyke late last night. Apparently he's been taping statements nonstop to avoid a long prison term."

Seth sat in his chair and leaned back. "What kind of statements?"

"Half-truths and some useful stuff."

"What half-truths?"

"Updyke swears he didn't kill any of the men here in Jasper. Said the worst he did was write 9-1-2 on Whitlock's hand as a warning to Savannah. We think he and Whitlock argued about killing Savannah, and Updyke killed Whitlock. He also said that Peter White was the one who sent him and Whitlock to Jasper."

Seth whistled long and low. "Any truth to that?"

Cody nodded. "A wire from a numbered account known to be controlled by the Rossis directly to Peter's credit card. It was a pretty decent way to hide the money, actually. No one thought to look at his credit card balances during routine checks."

"How did it work?" Seth asked.

"Peter got what looked like a credit placed on his card. A hundred grand a year, to be exact. Then he used the card or got cash advances and none of it showed up in his checking or savings accounts, which is what they check. At least we now know why he's been dragging his heels for six years."

"If he had this great thing going, why did he send two goons after Savannah?"

"The old man was ready to plead since he's dying. He asked Peter to do this one last thing for him to make his plea negotiations easier. Without Savannah, there was no evidence of the drug trafficking, which would have knocked out the RICO charge. Rossi could have easily been convicted of conspiracy to commit fraud, but at his age and since he's dying, a judge probably would have given him probation."

"So is there or isn't there a contract on Savannah?" Seth asked.

"No contract. With Peter and Rossi in custody, none of the underbosses are interested in her."

Seth grinned. "So she's free?"

"Yep," Cody said. "Or as free as she can be if Updyke is telling the truth."

"What truth?"

"He told this bull story about there being a shooter in the woods when they were waiting to kill Savannah down by the creek."

Seth smirked. "And this unidentified shooter is going to be his defense?"

"Oh, no," Cody said, laughing. "He described the guy. His description matched one of the characters on *Seinfeld*."

Seth suddenly had a horrible feeling flow through him. "What character?"

"George. Short, bald, glasses."

Seth cursed and grabbed the radio. Greg answered immediately.

"Is Savannah in the shop? Over."

"She hasn't gotten here yet. Over."

Cody and Seth rose in unison. Seth ran from the

office to Olive's shop. It was locked. He pounded on the door but got no answer.

He reared back and kicked the door in and raced inside.

"Olive!" he called several times as he took the steps to the second floor two at a time with Cody keeping pace.

They found her in bed, looking confused. "What on earth are you two doing up here?"

"Where's Junior?"

"He went out for a drive earlier," Olive explained. "He's been so busy with all his tax work that he wanted—"

"He came out to the ranch and took Savannah," Seth interrupted.

Olive struggled to a sitting position. "Then he must have wanted company. He loves her like a sister, you know."

Something in her tone disturbed Seth. "I don't think you get it," he said. "Junior is in a world of trouble. Where would he drive to?"

Olive shrugged, her expression vacant. "I don't know. But my son would never do anything wrong. He's always been a perfect boy."

"Where's your gun?" Seth asked.

"Gun?"

"There's a .22 registered to you. Where is it?"

"You'll have to ask Junior when he comes back. He keeps all the guns and rifles in his room."

Seth glared down at the woman and said, "For your sake, I hope Junior comes back. With Savannah."

"What do you mean?"

"I mean if he's taken Savannah and so much as a hair on her head is out of place, I'll exact some personal revenge before I arrest him."

Cody left the room and returned carrying three rifles. "Is this all of them?" he asked Olive. "There's no .22 in there."

"I'm not sure. Junior stopped going hunting after his father's accident."

Cody smelled the barrel of one of the guns and passed it to Seth to do the same.

"Well, someone fired this gun recently."

"That's not possible!" Olive exclaimed.

Cody bent the barrel and checked the chamber. "There's still one cartridge in here. Let's go see if they found one near Savannah's place last night."

"Wait!" Olive yelled, clearly panicked. "You can't punish my son. He's all I have."

"If he killed three people, the state will have him for some time."

AFTER DRIVING FOR HOURS, Junior pulled in front of a weathered log building that looked like a strong wind could blow over. The bushes were overgrown and a hunk of the chimney had crumbled. The only thing she could see were miles and miles of white-

peaked mountains and thick evergreens bordering a
strip on either side of the shack.

"What is this place?" she asked, forcing her tone
to convey interest.

"It was my father's hunting lodge."

That gave Savannah the creeps. She knew Frederick, Sr. had died from a hunting accident. *Had he
died in this shack? Would she?*

"Don't bother running," Junior warned. "It's
more than twenty miles in any direction before
you'd find another person. Most of them are recluses
and probably would shoot you as soon as help you."

"I wasn't thinking of running," Savannah lied.
"What do you want me to help you carry?"

Junior suddenly lashed out, slapping her hard on
her bruised cheek. "Stop it!"

Savannah tasted blood and touched her finger to
her already swelling lip. "Stop doing what?" she
asked.

"Pretending."

"I've never pretended with you, Junior. I've
always thought we were friends. Good ones."

"But not good enough for you to go out with me."

"You never asked," she pointed out.

"I couldn't!" he snapped. "Mother forbade it. She
thinks of you like a daughter."

"You still could have asked," Savannah said,
hoping to encourage him.

He shook his head so hard his thick glasses

slipped down his nose. He punched them back into place. "If I would have asked, she would have told. Everyone would know."

"So what? It wouldn't have mattered to me."

Junior hit her again. This time blood trickled from her mouth onto her blouse. "Just like you didn't care when the whole town knew you were having sex with Sheriff Landry? How do you think I felt, knowing how hard I worked to keep you pure? All the things I had to plan and do, and you ruined it by whoring yourself to a Landry."

When all else fails, there's always lying. "I haven't had sex with Seth."

Bad move. This time Junior hit her hard in the side. It knocked the wind out of her and felt as if he had cracked all her ribs. She had to get out of this car before he beat her to death.

"I'm cold, Junior. Can we go inside and build a fire?"

He pulled out a pair of handcuffs and attached one to her wrist and the other to the steering wheel. "I'll unload the car, then I'll come back for you."

To do what? she wondered. Maybe she didn't want to know the answer.

"THIS IS CRAZY!" Seth yelled. He was surrounded by all his brothers. Except for Clayton, for obvious reasons. They had set up a command center of sorts in the office at the Lucky 7.

Cody was on a cell phone, talking to the ballistics lab.

Sam and Shane were scanning maps of the area, trying to think of where Junior might drive. It had been almost eight hours since Junior had taken Savannah.

He had a deputy sitting with Olive in case Junior went home to Mommy. She was very angry and just kept repeating that her son was a good boy.

Seth looked out into the darkness and tried to quell the panic inside him.

Cody got off the phone and seemed upset. "They lifted a partial print of Frederick Baumgartner, Jr. off the Glock you recovered from Cal."

"Great, now we *know* he's a killer." Seth rubbed his face.

"Of men," Chance offered. "If he was killing her dates, then I think that means he wants her for himself."

The mere thought of Junior touching his beautiful Savannah made Seth's stomach turn. "So where would he take her to be alone?"

All the Landry men looked at one another but no one seemed to have a clue. "What about talking to his clients?" Sam suggested.

Seth nodded, called the deputy at Olive's and had him find and fax over copies of all Junior's clients and their phone numbers.

Twenty minutes later, the fax machine was

spewing out twelve pages. They divided them up, using cell phones, the fax line and the line into the house.

Unfortunately, Seth had Angelica on his list. He dialed her number and got Vincent.

"I'm looking for Junior Baumgartner," he said.

"He was here a few days ago, but I haven't seen him since."

"Listen, Vincent," Seth said in his most official tone. "If he was in the house, then he's the one who planted the gems in Ms. Seagal's studio."

"You mean Junior is the killer you've been looking for?"

"He's a suspect. And this morning he disappeared with Savannah Wyatt. Did Junior ever speak to you or Miss Seagal about a favorite place or someplace he liked to go when he was stressed or unhappy?"

Vincent didn't know of any such place, but put the phone down to go ask the mistress of the house. That too was a dead end.

Seth dialed the next name on the list. That client also had no idea where Junior might go.

"I heard he kidnapped that pretty girl from his mother's shop. Is that true?"

"Yes." Seth hung up and called the next number and the next, and the next. He continued to get non-answers. Apparently, wherever Junior liked to go, he kept it close to the vest.

"Olive has to know," Cody said. "I spoke to three

clients who had appointments with Junior yesterday. He canceled."

"And?" Seth asked.

"They covered the time of the shooting, including travel."

"So?"

"So it was Olive who told us that he had been out on appointments when you were shot. I read the police report on the Grayson shooting. Olive swore that Junior was with her at nine o'clock. I say we go gang up on her."

"DO I HAVE to be shackled?" Savannah asked. The chain and cuff he had pegged into the floor and attached to her ankle was painful. Just like her ribs and her mouth. Lord, how she wanted to get her hands around his thick neck, if for nothing else than for shooting Seth.

"Yes," he answered as he stood over the ancient sink and peeled vegetables. "I'm making stew, so I can't keep my eyes on you."

Savannah paced in a circular motion, which was all that her restraint allowed. The cabin was drafty and Junior had taken her coat and her shoes. She was freezing and couldn't get close enough to the fire to get warm. She knew that if she asked for privileges, Junior would either say no or hit her, hard. How had such an angry man hidden behind gentleness for so many years?

"Have you always been this angry?" Savannah asked when she couldn't stand the sound of him whistling as he cooked her dinner. It made it seem as if he thought she was a guest instead of a woman he'd kidnapped, beaten and now was freezing half to death.

"I had a difficult childhood," he answered. "My father died when I was thirteen."

"I know. I'm sure that was very difficult on you and your mother. It's one of the reasons you're so close."

Junior dropped the partially peeled carrot into the sink and came over to backhand her.

He hit her so hard that she landed on the cold wooden floor, banging her head hard enough to literally see stars.

"You don't know anything," he grumbled as he glared down at her.

Savannah curled into a fetal position, afraid he might kick her with the pointed toe of his cowboy boot.

"So explain it to me," she fairly pleaded.

"She didn't give me a chance," Junior said.

"Who? A girlfriend?"

"Mother."

"What didn't she give you a chance to do?"

"Anything, except be her personal servant and companion."

"Why?"

"Because she would have told the police what I did. Made it look like it was my idea from the start."

"Tell the police what, Junior?"

"That my father didn't die in a hunting accident. I shot him because she told me to." He pulled his foot back and kicked her, catching her in the tender upper thigh. "He was a good man but she didn't like being married. All of you women are like that. You act one way in public, then do other things in private. Just like you did with Seth."

Savannah reached into her pocket to rub her sore thigh. That's when she felt the small pill Chance had given her the night before. If she could knock Junior out, she could steal his keys and get herself away from the murderous lunatic. She just needed to figure out how to slip him the pill before he either raped her or killed her.

She wasn't sure which alternative was worse.

## Chapter Fifteen

The Landry brothers stormed Olive's Attic like an invading army.

"Why are you doing this to me?" Olive sobbed. "I haven't done anything."

"I beg to differ," Seth said. "We stopped on the way over here and checked out the evidence room at the courthouse. The same shell casings were found at Savannah's and at the site of your husband's supposed accidental death."

"It *was* an accident!"

"We'll know soon," Seth said. He motioned for J.D. to bring the portable fingerprint kit over.

"What are you going to do?"

"We found two sets of prints on the shell casings. One is Junior's, which have been on file since his father's death, but we don't have a match for the other set." He glared at her. "Yet."

Olive's motherly persona seemed to evaporate. Her eyes burned with hatred as she said, "Don't bother. I'm sure they're my prints. Frederick used to make me reload his shells for him."

"And you made enough for Junior to still have them around twenty-five years later?" Seth demanded.

"I told you, my son stopped hunting after the accident."

Cody stepped forward and said, "We're going to petition to have your husband dug up and reautopsied. I have a feeling we'll find evidence that it wasn't an accident. Forensics have changed a lot in a quarter century."

"What do you want from me?" Olive tearfully pleaded.

"The truth," Seth said. "You told me the night of Bill Grayson's murder that Junior was back home with you by nine."

"That's right, he was. We watched television together."

Seth bent down so that his arms rested on the arms of her chair. He was just a few inches from her face. "That's a lie and it makes you an accomplice to murder."

"Murder?"

"We have conclusive evidence that Junior killed Grayson. He escaped through the inn's ventilation system but he dropped something on the way out. Something with his fingerprints."

"Grayson provoked him," Olive now claimed. "He made several lewd comments about what he hoped would happen after his dinner with Savannah."

"And Whitlock?" Seth pressed. "What excuse do you have for that one?"

"He didn't do that," Olive insisted.

"Try again. We have a witness who identified him as the shooter."

Olive dropped her head into her hands. "This is all my fault."

"I'll make damned sure it is if you don't tell me where he has Savannah."

"You don't understand. He never would have killed those men if I hadn't set Savannah up on those dates. I didn't know how he really felt until after Bill Grayson died."

"He didn't just die," Seth challenged. "Your son killed him."

"Junior knew how men could be. He saw the way his father abused me. He was only trying to protect Savannah from unwanted advances."

"My advances weren't unwanted," Seth reminded her. "But he came within a few inches of making me an organ donor last night."

"He was just mad that you and Savannah had started something. He's been jealous of you for years."

"Over what?"

"Ruthie," Olive said. "They were friends and he knew that you were only using her just like his father had used me."

"Who actually killed your husband?" Sam asked.

Olive blinked. "I could never do anything like that. I needed Junior to help me."

All of the brothers looked at her with unbridled disgust. "You made your thirteen-year-old son kill his own father?"

"I couldn't live with Frederick. He wanted so much from me and I've had poor health my whole life."

"And what do you think Savannah's life is like right now?" Seth asked. "Is she even alive?"

SAVANNAH WAS shackle free while she joined Junior at a rickety table he'd set with candles and china she recognized as being from the shop.

The stew was warm, even if it wasn't one of her favorite foods. She didn't touch the chilled champagne. She was so cold her teeth were chattering.

"Drink up," Junior said. "I want you to be completely relaxed for later."

She almost gagged. This lunatic was going to play this like some seductive dinner, then rape her, then in all probability kill her just like he'd done to the others.

"I can't take anything cold, Junior. I'm freezing. May I please have my shoes?"

"Drink!"

Sensing noncompliance would result in more beating, she took a sip of the champagne. Then she downed the entire contents of the glass. If she was going to suffer, she'd rather not have all her faculties about her.

"That wasn't so hard, was it?" Junior asked, seemingly pleased.

"I would have preferred coffee," she said.

"After our meal," Junior promised as he refilled her glass and again ordered her to drink.

Two drinks in such a short period of time had an almost immediate effect on her. Her brain fogged and she was losing the ability to plan. Still, Junior gave her a third glass and this time she only sipped. She needed one or two of her wits to be in working order if she was going to get out of this.

Apparently she didn't anger him because he cleared the dishes and put an old-fashioned pot of coffee on the hot plate.

"Can we have coffee in the living room?" she asked. "By the fireplace?"

Junior considered her suggestion for some time, then nodded. He went to the worn sofa and arranged the pillows near the hearth. Then he took Savannah by the hand and arranged her on the pillows. When he reached for the top button of her blouse, she felt physically ill. Thankfully, he stopped unbuttoning it when her cleavage was visible.

Savannah's thoughts drifted back to the morning. To the sweet pleasures she'd shared with Seth. No matter what happened, *that* was going to be her definition of intimacy.

Junior went back to the hot plate and poured two cups of coffee, then brought them over to the hearth.

Savannah got an idea. "May I have some cream and sugar?"

Junior eyed her suspiciously. "You always drink it black."

"Unless I've had a full meal, then I like it light and sweet. Kind of like a dessert."

Junior hoisted himself off the pillows and took her cup back to where he had stored the cooler. Savannah knew this was her only chance. She also knew that if she blew it, she'd be dead in a matter of moments.

She split her attention between breaking the tablet into quarters and watching for Junior's return. If the things fizzed or smelled, she was dead.

He closed the cooler at the same instant she put the parts of the pill into his coffee. God must have been watching over her because they dropped to the bottom, where hopefully they would dissolve. Then it was just a matter of time. Assuming she had time left.

"SIX LANDRY BROTHERS?" Ruthie greeted with a huge smile. "To what do we owe this honor?"

"Junior Baumgartner," Seth said as he leaned across the counter. Olive said you two were friends."

"Were," Ruthie agreed. "When we were in our teens and early twenties. Why?"

"Junior is the one who has been killing Savannah's dates and he tried to kill me. He took Savannah more than twelve hours ago."

"Oh, my Lord!"

"Olive won't tell me where he might have taken her. I was hoping you would be able to help."

"He likes long drives," Ruthie said, obviously searching her memory. "He took Cal to an old cabin once when he was about ten."

"I know it's late," Seth began.

"Not for my son. I'll call him and see what he remembers." Ruthie was on the phone for less than ten seconds. "He's on his way."

"Junior has killed four people that we know of," he told Ruthie. "I don't want Cal coming along. It wouldn't be safe."

She shrugged. "There's six of you. He can take you there, but he can't give you directions. I'm counting on you guys to keep my kid safe. I know he's no angel, but he's extremely important to me."

"I'll take care of him," Chance offered. "I'll make sure he doesn't get in harm's way."

"Thanks."

Cal strolled in with an excited light in his blue eyes. "We're tracking a murderer, cool."

Seth looked at the boy. "Are you sure you can find the cabin? It's pitch-black out now. No moon, no nothing."

"Unless you're planning on driving without headlights, I can find it."

Lord, but the child was never without a smart retort. However, if it meant finding Savannah, Seth would put up with anything.

If he found her alive, he'd never let her out of his sight again. She was going to stay in Jasper and marry him if he had to drag her to the altar bound and gagged. All he had to do was find her.

"It's a pretty long ride," Cal said. "About an hour and a half if you do the speed limit." He grinned at Seth, apparently guessing they would break all land speed records to find the place.

"You be careful!" Ruthie called. In a slightly softer voice she added, "And safe, Seth. I saw instantly that you're in love with her. Don't lose that. I had it for a short time with Cal's father and I'm not sure you get a second chance in this lifetime."

Seth squeezed her hand and then led his crew out to the Bronco. He wondered how much time he could shave off the hour and a half.

SOME TRANQUILIZER, Savannah was thinking as Junior slathered her neck with wet, messy and repulsive kisses. He had finished the entire cup of coffee and since he hadn't beat her senseless, the pill must have dissolved.

So why wasn't he tranquil? she wondered. Maybe the coffee counteracted the pill.

"I'm hot," Junior slurred against her ear.

*I'm repulsed,* she wanted to reply.

Junior rolled away from her, which was a huge relief. His weight had been crushing her tender ribs. He was pinching the bridge of his nose, as if to clear a headache. She remained still, not fully sure if he was suffering the effects of the medication, or some other malady that would pass in a minute.

When he moaned, Savannah felt hope well up inside her. Very quietly, she rose to her knees and started backing away from him. Then she stopped. She couldn't get away without the car keys, which were probably in his pocket.

She grimaced as she pressed the back of her hand against his face. He didn't move. Next, she poked a single finger into his bare, protruding belly. Still nothing. Gathering her nerve, Savannah reached inside his right-hand pocket. She hit pay dirt. Slowly, so they didn't make noise, she began to extract the key ring from his pocket. She could just see the top of the ring when Junior's hand locked on her wrist.

Fear or something gave her added strength. At least enough to yank out of his hold.

"Savvannnah," Junior slurred angrily as he struggled to his feet and pulled out his gun. "Kill you. You did this to me."

She could stand there and get shot or she could

take her chances out in the elements. She had heard that dying of exposure was just like going to sleep. That sounded preferable to having Junior riddle her body with bullets.

She ran to the door and reached for the latch when the first shot rang out. It went through the door about two inches above her head. At least she had tranquilized his aim.

Rushing out the door, she ran blindly in the direction she thought was the road. Each step was like being cut with a knife. As she ran, she buttoned a few of the buttons on her shirt and tried to avoid as many low branches as possible. The soles of her feet were already getting numb and her lungs hurt from breathing in the frigid air.

She thought about stopping, then she heard a bullet whiz over her head. Glancing over her shoulder, she could just make out the weaving silhouette of Junior in his overcoat, not far behind her.

She was ready to cry when her body started to show signs of fatigue from exposure. She was slowing and Junior was gaining. Her feet were completely frozen and the rest of her wasn't far behind. It was getting difficult to put one foot in front of the other.

Savannah felt and tasted tears, amazed they didn't freeze on her face. She was going to die. It was kind of ironic, she thought as her mind began to wander. She'd spent six successful years hiding from one of the most dangerous crime families and she was going to end up dead at the hands of a deranged stalker.

She thought she saw a flash of light up ahead, but it disappeared so fast, she knew it had to be some sort of delusion.

"Savannah!" Junior was taunting her. She turned to see he was no more than twenty feet behind her.

He shot again and she felt pressure on her arm.

Then she heard another shot, but this one came from in front of her. She took two more steps and collapsed into a snowbank.

"Savannah!"

Hearing Seth's concerned voice, she tried to will her eyes open, but it just wouldn't happen. She knew he had lifted her because she felt the heat of his body.

"Ribs," she managed in a near whisper.

"Don't worry baby," he soothed. "I'll take care of you."

IT TURNED OUT THAT, all things considered, she was very lucky. Chance explained that her ordeal with Junior had left her with a through-and-through bullet wound in her right arm which was fractured, two cracked ribs, a bruised jaw, a black eye and a concussion.

"Hi," he said when he peeked into her room and found her awake. Seeing her so battered made him glad he'd killed Junior.

"Hi back. Sure you can stand to look at me?"

Seth moved over and kissed the end of her nose. It was one of the few nonbruised places on her body. Her arm was attached to some triangle thing above her head and he could see the blend of pain and medication in her striking eyes.

"I think you're beautiful."

"I *know* you're a liar," she laughed, then winced. "So are you going to fill me in?"

Seth carefully sat on the edge of her bed and gently stroked her hair away from her face.

"Junior is dead and Olive is in jail."

Tears formed in her eyes. "I'm not a very good judge of character, am I?"

"They had us all fooled."

"Did I hear Cody right? Is Peter White being charged with accepting bribes from the Rossi family?"

"Yep. Apparently the Feds got suspicious when they checked to see if your mother's work phone was tapped. When they found out it wasn't, they knew someone close to the case had to have told Whitlock and Updyke how to find you."

"Peter White agreed to help them kill me for a measly hundred grand? I'm offended."

"So was your mother."

Her face brightened. "You talked to my mother?"

"And your father and all three of your brothers."

"Where's my cell phone?' she asked. "I haven't talked to them in six years."

"Sorry, Chance has you on strict bed rest for the next four days. I'm only allowed in because I threatened to punch him in front of all his nurse groupies."

"Four days?" Savannah practically whined.

"You've waited six years, a few more days won't matter. I promise you, the minute I get you home, I'll hand you the phone and you can talk yourself a blue streak if you feel up to it."

"I definitely will take you up on that." Her expression changed. She looked sad. "I can't believe that four people are dead because of me."

"Because of Junior," Seth corrected. "And technically, one of those was mine."

"I guess I'm glad you're an expert shot."

He winked at her. "You might be surprised at how many things I'm an expert at."

With her swollen lip, she gave him half a wicked smile. "I know at least two things you're expert at."

"No talking dirty," Seth warned. "We need to start fresh."

"Seth," she began tentatively, "I want to go home to see my family."

"Okay."

"I don't know how long I'll stay," she said.

He tried to keep the hurt out of his expression. "I understand. But you have to do one thing for me before you leave."

"What?"

"Have dinner with all of us out at the ranch before

you leave. Your rescue was a joint effort and a lot of people would love to see you back on your feet before you go."

"Deal. When?"

"Two weeks? That way Chance tells me your face won't be swollen and your ribs will be less painful so you can be gently hugged."

"By you?"

"Among others."

"Are you sure we can't have a private party at your house in the meantime?" she suggested with a wink.

"Chance took those activities off your dance card for a couple of weeks. I'll be by to see you tomorrow." Seth kissed her head and slipped out of the room. He needed help, and he knew just who to ask.

IN TWO WEEKS Savannah still wasn't able to wash her own hair or tie a shoelace. However, aside from a few greenish smudges under her eye, her face was back to normal and her ribs didn't hurt. If only she could lose the blasted cast. She wasn't sure she could take four more weeks of this.

She knew she couldn't take much more of the new Seth. Incredulously, he acted as if their morning together at the ranch had never happened. He held her when they watched television, but he had her sleeping in the guest room of his house. It was as if something had extinguished all that passion.

She wondered if the something was knowing that Junior had touched her, even just a little. Maybe he held her somehow responsible for Junior's sexual impropriety.

Then there were the secret calls that he only took in his bedroom. It didn't take a rocket scientist to figure out they were probably from Ruthie.

She was supposed to be getting ready for dinner at the ranch, and she was growing more melancholy by the moment. She wanted to see her parents for a week or two, but then she had thought she would come back to Jasper to see if it could work between Seth and her. But in all the time since her ordeal, Seth hadn't once said he loved her, nor had he asked her to stay.

"So much for love at first sight," she grumbled. Well, maybe she'd try to give Seth a little going away present of her own.

Clutching the edges of her bathrobe together, she went to Seth's door and knocked.

"Yes?"

"I need some help getting dressed."

"Wear something more simple," he called through the door.

"No, this is a special occasion. Will you please help me?"

She heard a muffled sound, then Seth appeared and very nearly took her breath away. She had never seen him in a suit and it was a good thing, too. If she didn't have the blasted cast, she'd be doing her absolute best to seduce him right there. The charcoal raw silk accentuated his dark coloring and the monochrome shirt and tie made him look like the western version of a *GQ* ad.

Savannah purposefully placed herself in front of the mirror in the bathroom. She then pointed to the items she needed assistance with. Unbeknownst to Seth, she watched his every reaction in the reflection.

She dropped her robe and stood completely naked before him. She watched as his Adam's apple bobbed. Maybe he wasn't as immune as he was leading her to believe.

"The bra closes in the front."

Seth accomplished that with less than steady hands.

"Panties next."

He was chewing his lower lip.

"Those are thigh-high stockings, so just carefully pull them on for me, okay?"

"Sure."

There was a catch in his voice but he managed to get them on.

"Okay, now help me get this dress on and we'll be finished."

She had selected a short cocktail dress with a neckline that swooped off the right shoulder. When she turned so that he could slip it over her head and weave her cast through the opening she saw the tiny beads of sweat on his upper lip.

Her libido was in overdrive, but there was something very reassuring about knowing she still had an effect on him. A point he reinforced when he all but ran from the bathroom.

They left for the ranch a short time later. Their conversation on the way over included the weather, cattle futures and other unimportant items.

By the time they arrived, Savannah's earlier sense of triumph had all but vanished.

Seth took her good elbow and escorted her up the stairs. He pushed open the door and the foyer was dark. In fact, most of the house was dark.

Until Savannah started to walk past the dining room. Then the lights came on and scores of people yelled surprise.

If that wasn't enough to give her heart failure, seeing the five people in the front of the crowd was.

"Mom! Daddy! Guys!" She raced forward, hugging and kissing her family for the first time in eons. Her little brothers were now all taller than she was and her father's hair had started to go silver.

"This is a beautiful place sweetheart," her father said. "I think you made an excellent choice."

"Choice?"

Seth came up to her and took her hand. Shocking her beyond comprehension, he got down on one knee in front of practically the whole town and their respective families.

"Will you marry me?" he asked. He reached into

his jacket pocket and took out a black velvet case. Flipping it open, he showed her the largest diamond ring she'd seen on this side of a store window.

"I can't yet."

Her response drew a series of whispers and a horrified look from Seth.

"Can't or won't?" he asked, clearly embarrassed.

"I can and will, I just have to do something first."

"What?"

Reaching out, she cupped his upturned face. "I love you, Seth. Now that I've said it, I have to marry you. Call it Landry's Law."

* * * * *

*Fall in Love with...*

# MEN
## *in* UNIFORM

MUBPA10

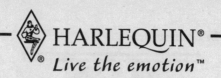

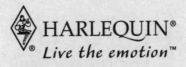

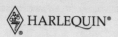

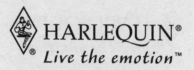

# HARLEQUIN®
# INTRIGUE®

## BREATHTAKING ROMANTIC SUSPENSE

Shared dangers and passions lead to electrifying romance and heart-stopping suspense!

Every month, you'll meet six new heroes who are guaranteed to make your spine tingle and your pulse pound. With them you'll enter into the exciting world of Harlequin Intrigue—where your life is on the line and so is your heart!

## THAT'S INTRIGUE—
## ROMANTIC SUSPENSE
## AT ITS BEST!

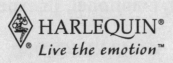

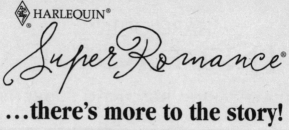

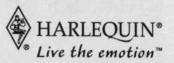